# His to Know

Book 3 in the His to Own series

Autumn Winchester

This is a work of fiction. Names, characters, places, and incidents are a product of the author's imagination.

Cover created by Covers by Combs

Edited by IFlowCreative

# Chapter 1

## Zachariah

The near-empty bottle of whiskey dangled from my hand, swaying back and forth. I watched in a drunken haze as the liquid sloshed around the edges of the glass bottle. It was mesmerizing. Or maybe I was just finally drunk enough to be entertained by just about anything at the moment.

Drinking dulled the feeling that was now residing inside my chest. I felt numb. Nothing could replace my dead soul. Nothing could fix what had been done. There was absolutely nothing left inside or out to fix the wrongs.

I was slowly drinking myself to death. I fucking begged for death to take me. My reason for living was gone. I knew I couldn't live past this heartache. There was nothing here to keep me going. My heart was broken into a million little pieces, scattered like broken glass from a horrific car wreck.

I couldn't wrap my mind around it. How could one even fathom doing so? The love of my life was gone. Fucking gone!

Before I was able to realize what I doing, I threw the whiskey bottle across the room. The sound of breaking glass did nothing to help my pent-up frustration. It only caused my blood to boil hotter.

I saw red.

Shoving everything off my desk angrily, the crash of the little things wasn't enough either. I needed *more*. Destroying the entire house wouldn't cure the fury that ran through my veins.

My heart rushed in frantic beats. My breaths labored. My thoughts consumed me. Everything was out of my control and there was nothing, anything or anyone would be able to do to make me stop.

My fists pounded into the wall. Hard. Fast. Unrelenting. Punch after punch, I hit whatever I could. My knuckles cried out in protest. But, I didn't stop. I *couldn't* as my haze grew.

Why? Why did she leave me? Didn't she know I'd do anything for her? Didn't Avidya know she was my world?

I knew I had to pull my shit together. I had to so I could go fucking find her. But pure agony filled the hole in my heart. There was nothing that could pull me away from my misery.

I had come home exactly one week ago, finding Avidya gone. She had packed a bag, leaving a tear stained note for me to find on the bed, right on the top of my pillow.

Her wedding ring sat on top as if *us* no longer mattered.

She was gone.

Some stupid fucker had called the brothel into the Feds, and within minutes, everything I had worked for was taken away from me. All the girls were taken into custody, some were taken to the hospital. Every man that worked there was taken into jail, and would most likely not be out anytime soon. It was their own fault that they were booked into jail. I paid them well enough that they had more than enough money to pay for a great lawyer.

I was more pissed off about the fact my wife left me without any warning, no excuses. There were no hints about her leaving, either.

I was held in custody for a little over four hours before my lawyer came and had me released. The brothel wasn't under my name, so nothing could be tied to me through any damn thing. The police had no reason to hold me any longer. I played dumb to any of the ongoings, and it worked well enough.

I had wisely switched all the legal papers over to Shemoli's name after he found his fate in death. It was a precaution if something were to happen, just like it had. I knew Shemoli would never be found, which was just what I wanted. Being the man that I am, I had to have backup plans for everything.

I knew that sooner or later, the brothel would be discovered, or someone would run their mouth to the wrong person. That, in turn, would lead to it being taken apart from the inside out. I was fucking pissed that my main source of income was ratted out, then turned upside down in so little time. Years of hard work wasted and thrown away like it meant nothing.

But what set me on my current downward spiral was my missing wife. She left me.

I knew my father was behind it. He gave me nothing, absolutely nothing, when I asked. He completely ignored me for a couple of days. I knew he was the one behind taking my wife. I just didn't know why. It wasn't like him, so why was my wife so fucking important that he took her from me? Did she ask for his help? Had he planned to take her from the first day he found about her?

Fuck!

I wouldn't think my father would do that. I didn't

think he'd take her away. So why? I had to find her, but where the fuck did she go? Where would I even start looking?

What the fuck had I done to make her leave me without a clear reason why? It just didn't make sense.

Dropping to the floor, I let out a gut-wrenching sob, letting my sorrow consume me. I ignored the pain as my knees hit the hardwood floor.

**~oOo~**

"Come on, son," my father grumbled, pulling me by my arm. He was easily able to pull my dead weight up. I wasn't helping him any; I didn't want to. What was the point?

"You can't drink yourself to death," he muttered as I flopped my body into the chair. My tingling feet felt like pins and needles with the few shuffled steps I was forced to take.

Huh. I was still in my office. How long had I been attached to the floor?

"Sure, I can," I slurred. I really fucking liked that idea. My eyes wouldn't stay focused, so I let them stay slightly open in a half slit.

8

"Not if I can help it," Dad said. His voice sounded like it was underwater.

As I forced my eyes open, everything was a blur. Halos appeared around the bright lamp on my desk.

I was beyond drunk.

*Shit!*

I couldn't recall the last time I was this drunk. I didn't think I ever had been. But hey! I couldn't feel a fucking thing, which was my motive. About time, too.

"Drink," Dad commanded, pressing something cold into my hands.

Hoping for something strong to keep my emotions at bay, I downed the liquid letting it soothe my parched throat.

"Water?" I asked in disgust. I hadn't wanted water.

"Yes. Water," Dad said as though I was a child. "Nothing else. You've drunk all the alcohol already. At least it saves me from having to dump it all."

"Why would you do that?" I asked, my voice weak from lack of use. Or maybe from being overused with all the yelling I'd done too many days in a row. I attempted to stand, but my body fell back into the seat. I wanted to save all my drinks from his hands. I had to have something around here still, somewhere.

Why would he dare throw away my precious alcohol?

"You know why," Dad deadpanned.

Had I asked my question out loud?

"You took my girl," I seethed, trying to glare at my father as he moved about in front of me. Well, I think he was moving. There were too many of him to follow whatever he was doing in my office.

"We'll talk when you are sober, Zach," he sighed out as though he was tired of my attitude. "Let's get you to bed."

"I ain't going anywhere," I slurred, letting my head fall against the chair. I refused to go to that room that my wife and I had slept in. I would rather sleep outside than that room ever again.

"Fine," Dad spoke, not fighting me. Wise choice on his end.

I let my eyes slide closed, too tired to try to fight it. All the whiskey and whatever other alcohol I consumed finally taking full effect.

## Chapter 2

### Avidya

Did I do the right thing? Was running going to be worth it? Would Zachariah hate me forever now? Would he try to find me? Would he succeed? What would happen if he did?

So many questions plagued my mind as I lay on the bed and stared out the window. The rain pelted against the panes of the glass, creating little rivers as the drops ran down the window pane. It felt like the sky was just as sad as I was.

I knew in my heart that I did, in fact, do the right thing. It was the only thing I could do to make sure the life inside of me would have a chance at life.

I knew logically that I had a few months before anyone would know that I was pregnant. I could have stayed with my husband longer. Maybe even get him to change his mind, or at least think about what the options were. But I was never good at keeping my worries to myself. Zachariah knew me too well. He'd either find out because my mouth splattered the news, or he'd have noticed my body changing. He was always too in tune with my body and my thoughts.

It didn't help that I tended to speak my mind without thinking first.

It would only have been a matter of time either way. I wouldn't be able to hide it from him. He was my world, and I never would keep such a thing from him, if I knew he wouldn't make me get rid of the issue.

With space, by all ways possible, I hoped—no, I prayed—that he'd see that I was doing the right thing. I wouldn't change my mind, no matter what he wanted.

I had no desire to be found anytime soon. That was the entire point of leaving with only a few belongings. I even left my wedding ring. It may have broken my heart to do so, but what other option did I have?

Behind me, the hinges of the door groaned in protest as it was pushed open. I remained staring off out the window, wondering about my choices as silent tears fell from my eyes. I felt as though that had been the only thing I had been doing the past week. It's all I *could* do as my heart tried to keep on beating.

"You need to eat," the man grunted awkwardly. I could picture him fidgeting in the doorway.

This man, although only welcoming me into his small house because of who I happened to be, tended to keep to himself. I wasn't sure if it was because of me keeping myself pretty much locked in this room, or because he didn't know what to do with a stranger in his home.

*Carlos had brought me here with little talk as I pretty much kept to my own thoughts the entire drive. We had only stopped a handful of times in the ten hours since I made that dreaded phone call to him.*

*He had made sure to keep all calls to his phone short and to the point when he happened to answer. He ignored the calls from his son and wife, knowing what they wanted. Who knows what would have happened if he'd have answered those.*

*I was positive that Zachariah was livid. At least we had a really good head start on my husband, despite what Zachariah was capable of.*

*When we arrived at the small tan colored house with a fairly greenish lawn, despite the late fall and crunchy leaves covering the ground, I wasn't sure what to expect. The lone leafless tree stood in the middle of the front yard.*

*A run down red pickup sat in the driveway. The paint was beginning to rust in places and looked like it was on its last leg of life.*

*"You should be safe here," Carlos stated as he shut*

*the car off, pulling the keys out of the ignition.*

*"Where are we?" I asked. I hadn't been exactly paying attention.*

*"Auburn, California," he answered. "Only Kent and myself know this man, or about him being here. This man here saved my life a few years back from someone that wanted me dead. He's very capable of keeping you safe if need be, along with helping you find everything you need."*

*"Okay," I yawned out.*

*It didn't take long to exit the car, Carlos carrying my bag as he led the way up to the front door. Less than a minute later, the door was pulled open, revealing the man that lived here.*

*Before his eyes landed on either one of us, they looked around the road and yard. After a quick second, they landed on Carlos. His dark black hair was pulled up into a top bun, a few pieces left out on purpose. Although his skin was clean shaven, this man was pretty much all muscle. He reminded me of a farmer or woodworker with how he held himself. He was dressed like a farmer with the cotton button-up, checkered long sleeved shirt and jeans he wore.*

*His dark eyes looked at Carlos through slits, as though he wasn't sure what our business here was.*

*"What do you need?" he asked darkly. His voice was rough, matching his exterior.*

*"I need your help," Carlos said as though he expected this man to do just that.*

*"Why would I want to do that?" the man asked, folding his arms over his chest. His entire frame filled the doorway.*

*"You owe me a favor," Carlos shrugged out as though it was that simple.*

*The man grunted, thinking the words over for a moment before finally stepping aside, letting us enter the house.*

*Once inside, I took an attentive look around. The wood floor was well worn but clean. The off-white walls of the living room held no pictures or personal mementos. Along one wall, next to the window, sat a light brown sofa. Across from it, was a fireplace with a TV mounted not far above.*

*The place felt homey, which I was not expecting. I hadn't been sure what I was expecting, but it wasn't this.*

*The man shut the door behind us, still basically not looking at me.*

*"So, what can I do?" he asked bitterly.*

*"I won't take much of your time," Carlos said.*

*"Avidya, this is Taylor. Taylor, Avidya."*

*The man, Taylor, nodded at me before returning his eyes back to Carlos.*

*"She needs to stay low for a while," Carlos stated.*

*"How long is a while?" Taylor asked. "I have things to do and can't be held up. You know I don't want to be dragged into your messes."*

*"Until she is ready to return," Carlos stated. "It's not my place to tell you her reasons. But she's not safe with my family."*

*"Why?" Taylor asked, glancing at me. His look was different than when he looked at the man that had brought me here. It almost looked like Taylor felt sorry for me.*

*"I'm pregnant," I stated. Surprisingly, my voice was even and didn't break, despite how much I'd been crying. "I can't stay there anymore."*

*"So, it's not his, then?" Taylor asked, almost knowingly.*

*"My son is the child's father," Carlos stated, a threat to his words. "He's not happy with his wife's choices. But Avidya doesn't want to do what Racheal did."*

*"Good," Taylor stated as though he didn't want that either. "She is welcome to stay for now. You make sure he doesn't show up here."*

"He won't," Carlos said, a sigh of relief with his words. "If so, you can deal with him how you like."

"Wouldn't do it any other way," Taylor grunted out. "I have a spare room. It's not much, but should work for now."

"Thank you," I whispered.

"It's what family is for," he shrugged. Then, turning back to Carlos, he asked, "How likely is it that he will show up here?"

"Not likely," Carlos said flatly. "You know I am one of only two people who know who you are, or where you are. You will both be safe here.

"Here," he stated, pulling a brown envelope from the inside of his coat pocket. "To cover any costs."

"That's not needed," Taylor said, waving it away.

"Fine," Carlos said, setting it atop the fireplace. "Just in case." He paused, thinking over his words as he turned to me. "You are doing the right thing, Avidya. Just do what you need to. When you are ready, you know where to call."

With that, Carlos left without a goodbye.

"I'll show you the room," Taylor croaked. I didn't argue as he showed to me the guest room.

And now, I found myself still in the bed barely

leaving it but for bathroom breaks as I was hardly eating anything.

"I'm not hungry," I muttered.

"If you want to waste away, go right ahead," Taylor grumbled. "You ran to keep that thing, you shouldn't give up on that. If that's what you're going to do, you might as well head back to that man you left."

"He'll kill it," I whimpered.

"And you will too if you don't get up and eat. You gotta take care of yourself if you expect to keep it," he huffed before leaving me alone once more. Unlike the last few times he had told me to eat, he left the door open. A clear sign that he expected me to get my butt up and take care of myself. Maybe he did care about my wellbeing.

He was right. I ran to keep this baby, I had to take care of myself to do so.

With a sigh, I pushed myself up and out of the bed. I couldn't let my efforts for running be wasted. I had to get things figured out, at least for a chance of life for the baby. It didn't matter if my heart was broken into a million tiny pieces. What mattered was keeping this little one safe and alive.

Once in the kitchen, Taylor already had a bowl of oatmeal set out, waiting for me.

"That wasn't so hard," he muttered, pleased that I finally was doing something.

"You have no idea," I said, slowly starting to eat.

"Oh, I think I do," he said. "A story for another time though. You, eat. Then we talk."

That didn't sound too good.

**~oOo~**

A huge yawn escaped my mouth as I finished off a second bowl of oatmeal and a side of strawberries. I was tired, but I guess crying almost nonstop for over a week would do that to anyone. Add on being pregnant, too, didn't help matters.

"So, who did you marry?" Taylor asked as he took the empty bowl and set it in the sink.

"Zachariah," I answered. A pang of guilt set in my gut at the mention of him. My voice broke over the one word.

"He's a bit old for you," Taylor said. He still had that roughness to his voice, but I think it was just who he was.

"I love him," I said. "I didn't pick him, exactly."

"Let me guess, Cody had something to do with

that," Taylor stated, not surprised.

"How do you know him?" I asked in way of an answer.

"He's my cousin. Well, was. I ain't got nothing to do with that family no more," he stated with haste. "I tried to get Racheal to let me have you, but yeah. That didn't work out well."

"Yeah, well . . . not like I had any say over any of it," I muttered. "Cody is dead. So is Racheal."

"Shame," Taylor said with a shake of his head. "I'd love to have a few words with that man. Anyhow, how was it that that boy got you, then?"

"He saved me, actually," I said. "Cody and Lynn had both been planning to have me kidnapped, but didn't know they were working against one another until it was too late. I got handed to Zachariah, and the rest is history." I summed it up. It didn't really matter what happened from then to now, did it?

"Huh," he huffed. "I never saw the youngest son to be soft, but I guess you are the one girl that causes fights in all families."

"Don't remind me," I said with a half laugh. "I'm tired of it all." I still had no idea why everyone kept fighting over me. I was just a simple girl that had been handed one crazy life.

"Don't blame you there," he replied. "So, why are you running from him if you love him?"

"He doesn't want kids," I said sadly, looking at my hands. "He said as much, and I know he'd do anything to make sure I didn't have any. I can't risk it."

"For you, he may change his mind," Taylor said. He seemed to think as though my husband would do that like switching a light on. It wasn't that easy; not when it came to my wants.

"A fat chance in hell on that," I said. "He thinks killing an unborn baby is right. I can't allow that to happen. Cody may have forced God on me, but I still believe killing is wrong. Even within a mafia family."

"Sorry to break it to you, kiddo. But mafia families kill. They don't care who you are," Taylor stated flat out.

"The less I know, the better," I yawned.

"I work the night shift. Will you be okay on your own?" Taylor asked.

"I'll manage," I grimaced.

"Here's an extra cell I have. I have my number entered," he said, pushing a black flip phone my way across the table to me. "There's a gun in the safe under my bed and it's left unlocked if you need it."

"I don't know how to use one," I said, my eyes wide. Was he expecting something to happen?

"No worries about that," he shrugged. "Anyone that comes by won't know that. I'll be back by six in the morning. Keep the doors locked, shades closed. No one will know you are here. Not like my neighbors like me much as it is."

"Oh, why's that?" I asked.

"I don't like them," was his answer.

"You don't like anyone, do you?" my mouth ran off again.

"No," he stated. He seemed to want to say more. Instead, he turned and put coffee in a thermos.

He didn't seem like the talking type, but maybe he just had a soft spot for his chosen family. I was, after all, put into this mess by fate. I didn't have many choices in anything.

I watched him from the table as he got everything ready for work. I almost wanted to ask what he did, but decided against it. I didn't want to make him mad.

"You sure you'll be okay?" he asked again.

"I can take care of myself," I grumbled. "I'll just go back to bed."

He grunted through his nose as if he was afraid to

leave me here. Should I have been more afraid to be left in some stranger's house? Surely Carlos wouldn't have left me here if it wasn't safe for me to be left entirely alone.

Five minutes later, I was left alone in the house. I felt out of place being here. Maybe I shouldn't have come here. Maybe I should have just stayed and faced the consequences with Zachariah.

It was too late to doubt that now. I was here, after all. And somehow, I was able to find the will to get my lazy butt up and take a shower. I couldn't remember the last time I took a shower, as the days had all blended together in the past week.

In the shower, I let all my worries, for now at least, be washed away. My heart may be broken, but I had to do what was right. I had to take care of the little baby, to give it a life that it needed to survive in this world. I refused to let this choice be the end of my life, or the one inside of me.

I just hoped that my emotions didn't take over and make me second guess everything.

## Chapter 3

## Zachariah

I felt like utter shit. My elbows were on the counter, my head in my hands as my mother busied herself with making food. My head pounded so horribly, I thought it was going to explode. It didn't help when my mother thought it was necessary to slam every cupboard she opened, and banging the pans around.

I blamed my father. I wouldn't feel like this if he'd just let me drink myself to death. It would have been a lot easier. Or at least let me keep drinking to numb the pain. Or if he'd just fucking answer one of my many questions.

"Would you knock that off!" I hissed as my mother dropped the pan again on the counter. I swear she was doing it on purpose. Oh wait—she was.

"Don't you dare," she hissed right back, not afraid of me. "Serves you right for your unwise choice."

I clamped my mouth shut, knowing she'd only make it worse if I said anything more. It wasn't often that I was hungover. But the times I was, my lovely mother always made sure to bang every blasted thing. I was sure it had more to do with the fact that I should know better.

She would even do it when it came to my father.

Speaking of him, I was currently not talking to him. There was no way he'd get his say in any of this. He took my wife, even if she asked, away from me. He wouldn't give me answers that I had to have. My father was not just one of the men I could do as I pleased with. I couldn't just shoot at him and get what I needed. With Carlos, I would have been shot back at, or worse, killed for even daring to do such a thing as that.

"So why are you ignoring your father? He won't tell me much of what is going on, but I'm not the one giving him the cold shoulder," my mom hinted, sliding a plate of food my way.

"You know why," I grumbled. "He took Avidya." That was the only answer he had given me after I pretty much pushed him against a wall for at least one answer. It didn't help matters for either of us. I wanted my wife back and I knew that my father was the only man that could make that happen at the moment. It wouldn't stop me from tearing the entire earth apart to find her, though.

"She asked to be taken," Mom stated sadly. "She has her reasons."

"Which you don't know of," I huffed.

"This is one of those things where the less I know,

the better. Your father wouldn't tell me if I were to ask anyhow. She wanted out, and that is all there is to know," Mom explained. "She'll come back when she's good and ready."

"Why? That's what I don't fucking get!" I hissed.

"Watch it," Dad spat my way as he entered the kitchen. He had cleaned up the office, the one that had been completely destroyed by me just hours ago. I would have just left it, reminding myself of what a huge failure I was to my wife. "I won't put up with you talking to your mother like that."

I glared at him, daring him to do anything to me. It was completely his fault. I clenched my sore fists, feeling the cracked skin sting in protest. I nearly broke one hand from my tantrum. I did deserve it.

"She's safe, right?" Mom asked.

"As safe as she was here," Dad answered. "She'll be fine, though. I trust the people I left her with."

"Which is where?" I asked, hoping beyond hope my question would be answered.

"Somewhere," Dad answered. "She doesn't want you to know."

"Why can't you just fucking tell me?" I seethed before storming off. I ignored my mom's concerned voice floating after me.

Of course, my father just had to follow me. Again. What did he think I was going to do? All my whiskey was gone, so I couldn't go back to drinking away my problems.

"Go away," I muttered as I went upstairs. I just wanted to be left alone.

"Not till we have a little chat, son," he said. I knew that tone of voice. The voice that meant he wasn't going to put up with my shit. Too bad for him. He'd deal with it until he brought back my wife. I was not going to let him have that option of controlling me like a toddler.

"Well, that isn't going be happening," I stated.

"It is," he said, his voice turning into the demanding mobster that I knew him to be. "You will listen, and you will obey my orders."

"Or what?" I laughed, not afraid of this man.

"Then I'll make damn sure that your wife never does return to you. I'm sure with time, she'd rethink her actions. But I can certainly make sure that she doesn't," he threatened.

Oh? He thought he could just threaten me like that? Really? Did my father think he had that much power over one person that had nothing to bargain with?

"I'll find her on my own then," I snapped.

"No, you won't," he said, amused that I even thought that. "Guess I can always just make sure she knows that you won't ever change your ways."

Was he goading me? Really?

"What the fuck do you want?" I said, turning around without warning. My dark eyes blazed with hatred and fury at this man I called my father.

"I told you," he said calmly. He waited for a moment before speaking again. "Are you ready to listen?"

"You don't give me much choice," I stated harshly.

"Alright," he sighed, running a hand down his face. "You are going to get cleaned up. Since your main income source is no longer up and running, you will put your efforts into that club of yours. You will keep money coming in. You *will* live, and be ready for when your wife returns. And you will keep an open mind when she does."

"You think running my club is going to change anything?" I asked, not getting what he was trying to do. Who cared what kind of money I brought in anymore?

"No," he said through his nose. "It'll give you something to do. You can't wallow in self-misery. You will get things back in order and live life like you did before she ever came into our lives."

"For what? So, she can see I don't want her? So she

can see just how fucked this family is?" I asked sarcastically. At least I was no longer filled with heartbreak. Pure anger ran through my body as hot as ever. "I am not going back to how things were before her. There is no chance in Hell that I will do that. Ever."

I hadn't known what I was missing until I had it.

"You will keep on living to make sure you have something for her when she returns," Dad stated.

"There's no point!" I yelled, my voice echoing in my ringing ears. "She left me. You won't tell me why, or where she went. She won't be back unless I drag her ass back here. Then I'll whip said ass so much she won't ever think about running again."

Before I knew what happened, my father's fist hit my face with such force, I was knocked sideways into the wall. My hand clenched at my side as I glared daggers at the man. My heart beating rapidly inside my chest.

"You will never raise a hand to her," Dad seethed. "And if you keep up that line of thinking, I won't bring her back. It won't matter that our entire family is heartbroken by her leaving."

With that, he turned and left me in the hallway, steaming with anger and shock.

He had never hit me before. My father had never

raised his hand to me. Ever. Even with being a man of power, the Don of this family, he had never raised a hand in anger at any of his family members.

Until now.

## Chapter 5

### Avidya

I swear I had just fallen asleep when I was being shaken awake. The shaking was so bad that the entire bed was moving with the force.

Was there possibly an earthquake?

No. The hand on my shoulder was a good indication that was not happening.

With a low groan, I forced my eyes open. The first thing I saw, other than it being way too bright outside, was Taylor as he stood over me. I stared up at him, confused as to why he was waking me up. I was sleeping so well, too. Why couldn't he just let me sleep?

"You have a visitor," he grunted, not seeming happy about that fact.

"Huh?" I muttered, trying to rub away the sleep and the fogginess that covered my brain. This man was going to learn quickly that I was not a morning person. It had gotten worse the past few weeks, too. I wasn't an *anything* type of person, truthfully.

"You have a visitor," he repeated, a bit slower this time. His hard voice turned into slight amusement.

"Who?" I asked after a moment as the words registered. Who would possibly come here?

"I guess you'll have to see," he said, leaving me to myself.

Thoughts of my husband instantly filled my head. I was sure it wasn't him, since he'd most likely just charge in here without a second thought. Plus, Taylor didn't seem to be a huge fan of the man. There was no one outside of a very few limited people that knew I was here, and I figured it would have stayed that way.

With a long sigh, I slowly pushed myself up and out of the bed. This bed wasn't as soft or as welcoming as the one at Zachariah's house, but it was good enough. The bedroom had a full-sized bed, a tall six-drawer dresser, a window looking out to the back yard, and once more, nothing personal. All my belonging easily fit in the closet. Not that I had taken the time to unpack just yet. A plus side to it was that I was right next door to the bathroom.

After using the shared bathroom, I slowly made my way towards the living room and kitchen. I didn't bother getting dressed, or brushing my hair. I had no one to impress, so I didn't see the point.

I may be eating now, but that didn't mean I was trying the best that I could to keep things as if nothing had changed. My heart was still in millions of pieces. I was broken, and forever would be. I would eat enough just to get by, my appetite nearly nonexistent as it was.

Pausing before entering the living room, I wasn't sure how to react. Nor what to say. I assumed this wasn't a simple social call, given I have been here for only a little over a week. I never expected to see him, at least not here of all the places he could have shown up.

"Kent," I said with a nod of my head his way. My voice came out emotionless as I hid my worry.

"Hello, Avidya," he replied in kind. He took a moment to look me over as I stood there, fidgeting. Yeah, I wasn't impressed with my own appearance, but it was the least of my concerns at the moment.

"I'll just go out back," Taylor stated, feeling as awkward as I was I'm sure. I had quickly found out that Taylor didn't like change. I didn't care much for it myself most of the time.

It hadn't been all that long ago with Kent and I were able to get along fairly well. It was during that time when Zachariah was in the hospital, but I had hardly seen this man since then. My husband and I had been a bit busy dealing with life. Now, I wasn't so sure how to behave in the presence of this man.

"So, it's true?" Kent asked, not walking around the subject.

I shrugged, willing tears to not come to my eyes. Many things were true these days. "Depends on you are asking me."

His eyes moved to my stomach, seeming to try to calculate things in his mind. I wasn't showing yet, but that didn't stop him from saying what he wanted.

"Are you sure? I can talk to my grandson about this, you know," Kent stated, raising his eyes back to mine.

"There is nothing on this earth that will change his mind. Zachariah has said what he will force me to do if I became…well, this," I said, hot anger flashing behind my eyes. I moved one hand up and down my body in a manner that spoke what my words were unable to. "This is the only thing I can do."

"Alright," Kent said. He didn't argue. I figured he may have wanted to since I was carrying his great-grandchild.

Once more, I couldn't help but notice just how much the male gene took effect in this family. I knew for a fact that when Zachariah was old and gray, he'd look like Kent's twin. Dark brown eyes, dark hair with gray, and slightly wrinkled skin around the eyes and mouth. Kent looked good for his age, that was for sure.

"I had to see for myself," Kent went on. "Zach isn't doing well." Why he made sure to tell me, I wasn't sure. What was the point in even telling me? To make me feel worse than I already was?

"You think I am doing any better?" I asked with a huff. "Sorry, I'm not a morning person." I took a deep breath, willing my anger at the situation to leave me.

"I think you are entitled to it," Kent laughed. "That man of yours is going to hate me, but I think you did the right thing. Zach has always been stuck on the rules he made for himself. You need to get a doctor lined up. And how long do you plan to stay away? Julia sends her well wishes."

"You mean she knows you are here?" I asked, surprised.

"Well, no," he said slowly. "But I'm sure she would all the same."

He didn't seem sorry that Julia, nor anyone else for that matter, didn't know I was here.

"I don't know how long I'll be away," I answered. "I want to keep the baby. I can't be like my parents, either set of them. I can't stand by and let someone raise my child." My vision clouded with tears, but I forced them away. I had to stop crying over everything.

"You'll need a job," Kent hinted.

"I know," I sighed. I knew I had to get myself in order to search for a job, a place to stay, and everything else I needed.

"Taylor will help you out," Kent went on. "Do you know who he is to you?"

"Since she's been in the bedroom pretty much the entire time she's been here, not really. We haven't really talked," Taylor answered. "She knows that we are related."

"Eavesdropping?" I laughed.

Taylor simply shrugged, not sorry for doing so. "It's my house." He paused, thinking something over. Finally, after a full minute, he spoke. His voice was softer, almost like he was afraid to say what he was saying. "You are welcome to stay here, Avidya. There is more than enough room. At least until you know for sure what you want to do. Carlos entrusted me to keep you safe, and I will do that by any means necessary."

"You will be safe here," Kent agreed. "No one comes to this little town."

"Haven't had any issues all the years I've been here," Taylor mused.

"The reason I came here," Kent said after a

moment. "Is because I have these bank cards and IDs for you, Avidya. Can't go by your known last name." He motioned to an envelope that sat on the table. "I'll transfer some funds into the bank account monthly, so you can get what you need."

"Then why does she need a job?" Taylor asked, taking a seat on the couch.

"To give her purpose. To make friends. To get out of the house," Kent shrugged. "Why do you have a job, Taylor? Would it be the same reasons?"

Taylor grunted some sort of reply, and Kent shook his head.

"Sorry, you were left with this meathead. Really not sure what my son was thinking, but at least you won't be known here," Kent laughed.

"I just don't like people," Taylor grunted out, eyeing the man.

Yeah, I didn't much care for people either. I liked it here so far. So that had to be a plus, right?

I did have to wonder what the history between these two men was. They seemed to only tolerate each other because they had no other choice. And that could be the whole reason Taylor wasn't too happy about the Melendez family.

## Chapter 6

### Avidya

Fully awake now that Kent had left as quickly as he had shown up, I took a seat on the other side of the couch. My mind was reeling with questions once more. None of which I was willing to ask out loud. I didn't want to know the answers to my questions. I was more than happy to not have answers that would no doubt lead to even more questions that wouldn't be answered any time soon.

What was I going to do? Could I really stay here that long with this man? *Who* was this man to me? Would we both be safe here, even after the baby came? And what would become of me after that? Would I be able to just go back like nothing had happened with a baby in tow? Would everyone just accept us both as if nothing had happened?

"You okay?" Taylor asked, glancing my way.

"Yeah," I muttered, shaking myself away from the thoughts that began to plague me. It didn't seem that my husband was faring all that much better than me. He was depressed and wanted to find me. Kent said he'd do whatever he could to make sure that Zachariah would stay as far away as possible, keeping him busy with business and family stuff.

How long would that last?

I wasn't sure if Zachariah feeling as horrible about my choices as I was was a good thing or not. I was happy to know that he wasn't pissed off at me, but instead worried. Would we both be able to get past this and move on; to keep on living as though we never knew each other? Or would fate somehow bring us both back together one random day?

We were both heartbroken, and only I held the power to fix that. Now was not the time to try. That was for sure.

"So, who are you, exactly?" I finally asked, not sure if I wanted to know that answer. I raised my eyes to meet his, the same eyes that I had seen countless of times on another man I refused to really think about here and now. "Taylor Shantez. I was once a Hartwell, but that was over twenty-five years ago," he answered. I'm Aaron's brother, but he can rot in hell with the rest of them," Taylor grunted. It didn't seem like anyone liked that man. The one and only man that wanted me dead, so, it seemed.

I remembered this man's name, and now things were beginning to click into place. I vaguely remembered seeing him in a picture, but it was quite a while ago so I couldn't remember as well.

"No one ever talked about you. Travis mentioned looking for you but didn't have any luck in doing so," I mused. It was on the trip he took before I was kidnapped. I remembered how angry I was at Travis when he did return from his little so-called trip.

"Ah, yes," he huffed in a partial half laugh. "Travis is smart, and that'll get him into trouble soon enough."

"He means well, though," I said. "He's been helpful the last few months. Along with his…girlfriend." I wasn't sure what to call Keena, but I guessed girlfriend was close enough. I didn't want to say something that made Taylor uncomfortable with the entire lifestyle I had been thrown into. Just because I was accepting of such things didn't mean everyone else was.

"At least someone is," Taylor grunted out.

We lapsed into silence once more. It wasn't uncomfortable, but it also felt strange. I was trying to understand this man, understand his past and present at the same time. He was standoffish, yet in a careful sort of way. I could understand it.

"Where is Cody at these days?" Taylor asked.

"Dead," I stated, not feeling bad about it either. "He

broke into our home and Zach's guards took care of him. That was after scaring the crap out of me."

"That would be certainly a death sentence," Taylor spoke, not seeming all that surprised. "He never was too smart. Thought his God could save him."

"You don't believe in God?" I asked, surprised.

"I do," he said slowly. "Just...I'm not in the best place with him after all these years. God has never worked in my favor, girl."

"Why's that?' I asked, generally curious. I turned, putting one leg underneath me so I faced Taylor.

"I have just been dealt a crappy hand in life," he said as a way of explanation. "It really doesn't matter how, or why. It is as it is."

"I'm a good listener," I stated.

"You don't want to hear of my sorrows, girl. It's in the past, and that will be where it all stays," he said, keeping his eyes on the TV the entire time.

"If you change your mind..." I trailed off.

"Why didn't you go to college? You'd make a great psychologist," he hinted, changing the subject.

"Cody," I shrugged, feeling it was enough of an explanation. "And now, that's not an option. I have enough to deal with."

He nodded his head, as though it made sense. I could see his mind working on a way to try to convince me of maybe at least trying out college, but I didn't want to hear it.

After having to make sure I had straight As all through school, I was done having to spend hours upon hours to make sure I kept studying and making sure I was the perfect daughter Cody wanted. I had to have perfect grades, and I hated it. I hated spending so much time on school work when there was life to explore out in the world. There was no way I'd ever willing do that again.

What did it matter if I was the best at school work when I was meant to be married off? I couldn't have been happier that I came to be in Zachariah's hands when I did.

"Shouldn't you be sleeping?" I asked, remembering he worked last night. I also noticed it was now early afternoon. I must have been very tired to sleep so late.

"I was able to get my schedule switched. Don't want to be leaving you alone at night in case something happens," he answered.

I was sure he did that for me, but I kept that to myself. I saw how he tried to show that he didn't care about me even though he did. It was almost sweet that he did care. His gruff exterior was just for show, and after so many years of most likely trying to put anyone off, he had no idea how to really be anything else.

I could relate more than I liked to admit. I wasn't sure how to get along with people. I didn't know how to connect and keep a relationship with hardly anyone. The only person I ever could really get along with without having to try was Becca. That was taken away the same night I was taken away from everything I had once known.

Things had changed so much the past couple of years. So much so, I didn't even know who I was. I had thought I had that part figured out, but then things changed once more. It always seemed to when I didn't want it.

Just another thing I had to figure out. At least I wasn't alone in this. I could see that Taylor struggled with life more than I did. I hoped that with us together, I could get him to see the bright side of life. I needed to, and I couldn't do it alone.

# Chapter 7

## Zachariah

I was anything but happy as I sat at the bar, overlooking the club area. I detested being here. I would rather be in jail then right here at the moment. I didn't want to see all these happy couples. I didn't want to hear about how happy a Dom was with his sub. Least of all, I didn't want to hear all the happy emotions that came with sex around me.

I just fucking wanted to go home to me in my own misery without having to be around anyone.

I was only here to appease my father. He really hadn't thought through me being here. There was alcohol. And someone that I could easily find to help numb my pain. He had to know that I would do anything to keep my feelings at bay for as long as possible.

The only thing stopping me from doing either of those things was knowing I'd never cheat on my wife, even if she thought what we had was over. And the bartender was Travis, who refused to serve me anything but water. That fact didn't make me any happier, either.

Yes. I was glaring at everyone around me. No one

dared to come up to me because of that.

Thank fuck for that. I wasn't in the mood to be my normal sociable self.

"You aren't too sociable tonight," one of the regular Doms spoke, sitting down next to me. His buzz cut and sharp jaw stuck out every time I looked at this man. He was polite and respectful, which is how he got into my club a little over a year ago. He followed the rules, never stepping over that line that was easily crossed by many.

"His girl left him," Travis stated easily, passing Bruce the drink he had asked for.

"That sucks," he hummed out. "Go find another."

"I'm still married," I muttered, running a hand down my face. The ring on my finger should have been a clear sign that I wasn't giving up on my wife. I never would.

"Well, she still left. To me, that means she is no longer in the picture. At all. You have free reign, man," Bruce laughed.

"Still not going to," I seethed, glaring at him.

"Then find a Dom that will take the pain away. It works just as well," Bruce stated.

"That won't work either," Travis said, saving me from having to reply. Tempting as it sounded, I knew I couldn't do that either. I'd hate if Avidya went to someone else if I had left her, just like she left me. I may be hurting, but I would go that far to take my pain away. Whiskey worked just as well, for the most part.

"Well, good luck, buddy," Bruce said before standing and looking for a sub to play with.

He was the type that only wanted a plaything, switching constantly from one to the next. He was a great Dom; I had to give him that. No woman ever complained about him not following the rules in this establishment.

"How about you just go to the office. I don't need you here. You'll just dampen the mood," Travis said, shooting me an irritated look.

That sounded like something I could do. It was much better than sitting here having to socialize. I did just that, too. It was better than sitting in the middle of people who I had no desire to even talk to.

I had wanted to once bring my girl here on a night like this. I wanted to show her just how much of my world she could like and crave. I wanted to show her that this life that I lived was exciting. Now, that chance was gone. I hadn't heard a thing from her, or about her. I was even trailing my father to see if he would go visit her, and nothing.

Not a damn thing.

No one in my family went anywhere out of the ordinary. There was nothing to lead me where my wife was. I hated it. Everyone around me knew I hated it, too. It wasn't a secret, that was for sure. Truthfully, I wasn't sure how they were still able to be around my ass with my angry filled hate that I was showing everyone lately.

Maybe my father was right. Maybe Avidya would come back after she got her thoughts in order. I still didn't know why she left. That was what kept bugging me. If only I knew, I could just do something to fix it!

Nothing could fix the giant hole in my chest from her leaving me. There was absolutely nothing that could fix that but her. Didn't she know how much I fucking loved her? Didn't she know that she'd take my heart with her if she ever left?

Sitting at my desk, I couldn't help but miss my wife more with each passing minute. I felt like I could never overcome her leaving me.

Why?

Why did she leave? Why couldn't she just come talk to me?

*Why, God damn it!*

I rested my head in my hands, forcing the tears of

destruction away.

I would find her. I would bring her back, kicking and screaming if I had to. I would go to the ends of this earth to get her to see reason.

I'd even tie her up to make her listen if I had to.

I was a monster. And that monster was just unleashed.

# Chapter 8

## Avidya

Within days, I sat at the doctor's office, my knee bouncing as I sat in the chair. I wasn't sure what would happen, but I knew I had to get this done. I had to get it confirmed.

What if I wasn't really pregnant? What would I do then? Was there any chance that I wasn't?

I was sure that if I went by periodic vomiting episodes, I was without a doubt pregnant. So why was I second guessing that positive test? I had no idea. I was getting pretty good at second guessing everything these days.

Maybe I should have let Taylor tag along to this, just so I didn't have to go alone. But what was done, was done. There was nothing I could do to change it now.

Looking around the waiting room, I was nearly by myself. The walls were painted a soft cream color, matching the blackish gray chairs that were set up around the waiting room. In the corner that was along the same wall as the entrance door, there was a small table with four colorful chairs around a blue round table. A few coloring books and markers set on the table in the middle. Next to that, was a small bookshelf filled with books.

Apparently, this was one of the best doctor's offices in town. Although, there was only one other one not all that far away.

The only other person besides the receptionist was an older lady who was currently looking through some house décor magazine, humming to herself.

It wasn't that long of a wait before my name was called by a nurse who wore SpongeBob scrubs. I stood, following her past the door and into what looked to be a hallway.

"Have you left a urine sample?" she asked, looking at the chart in her hands.

"Yes," I answered. That was the first thing asked of me after I filled out the forms, using my borrowed name and address. It had felt weird, though. In a span of six months, I now have had three different last names. What more could possibly change?

"Good," the nurse stated. "Please, step up onto the scale."

I did as instructed, letting the nurse weigh and take my blood pressure. She seemed to want to get done with her day, and I couldn't blame here. She looked tired and worn down.

After showing me to the room, she said the doctor would be in shortly.

I took a seat on the examination table, the white paper crinkling as I tried to get comfortable. I never did understand why they had to use this type of paper.

After waiting for nearly three minutes, there was a soft knock on the door before it was pushed open.

"Good afternoon, Miss Shantex," she greeted. Her hair was pulled back by clips on both sides of her face, making her square face more prominent. Her bright blue eyes looked me over. "I'm Dr. Fare, but please call me Ree. I see you are here to confirm being pregnant."

"Ah, yeah," I said. My voice came out a bit quieter than I had hoped. My hands were damp with sweat.

"No need to be nervous," she stated, taking a seat on a purple leather stool. "The sample you left confirms you are, indeed, pregnant. Any idea how far along you may be?"

"Not really," I grimaced. "It wasn't planned."

"That's perfectly fine," she spoke. "Before I come up with a plan of action, I'd like to do an ultrasound to find out how far along you are."

"Okay?" I said, figuring that much.

"What are your plans?" she asked, folding her hands in her lap, giving me her entire attention.

When I didn't answer right away, she explained a bit more. "Do you plan to keep the baby?"

"Yes," I answered. Why else would I be here?

"Is the father in the picture?" she asked next.

"No," I said, shaking my head. "He doesn't know, nor will he."

"Okay," she said, not asking for clarification on what I said. "Last one. Do you want to know the gender when that time comes?"

"Yes, please," I laughed. It'd be a bit easier to figure out how to live my life if I knew what would be in store.

"Perfect," she replied easily. "Everything will work out just fine. I can answer any questions that you have. All new moms, and even experienced ones, always have a question or two. Now, I'd like to get that ultrasound done today if possible, just to get an idea on how far along you are. You'll need to start taking prenatal vitamins, along with making sure you take care of yourself.

"I'll have a nurse draw some blood to check iron levels and the works while I check to see if our lab tech is in," she finished. "Any questions?"

I shook my head, trying to grasp everything she had said.

"If you do, let me know. I'll also have a packet of stuff for you to look and read through that will help you. Along with a pregnancy book that should also help you with anything that will come along."

With that, she left the room, leaving me to muse over her words.

I could do this, right?

~oOo~

"Everything good?" Taylor asked as I slipped into the passenger seat of the pickup.

"Yep," I said, still in a daze. I sat the folder of information in the space between us before buckling my seat belt.

"You okay?" he asked, turning his eyes to me. His voice was softer as he asked the question. Was he scared I was changing my mind on my reasons, on my beliefs?

"I'm pregnant," I stated, my voice quiet.

"That is why you are here," he said, trying to hide his amusement.

"What will I do?" I said more to myself than to him. I hated feeling so out of whack, overwhelmed, and just plain out tired.

Taylor didn't answer me, knowing I wasn't looking for an answer from him. Instead, he gave me a small smile and started the truck. Backing out of the parking lot and out onto the street.

"I wish he'd be here," I muttered. "I wish Zach could experience all this. But most of all, I just wish he'd not hate the idea of having a kid."

"I'll be happy to tag along with you to your appointments, if you want me to, that is," Taylor said. His words were quiet, but I heard them all the same.

"You don't really want to," I said, leaning my head against the window. "Plus, you have to take time off of work."

"Have to do that anyhow," he grunted. "I don't mind."

"You sure?" I asked, looking at him.

Although he was nervous and didn't really wanting to go to every single appointment with me, he would. Not because he was obligated to keep an eye on me, but because he really did care.

"What else do I have to do?" he shrugged in an

answer. "It's what families do. I may not have been there for you when you were a child, but I sure as fuck will try now."

"Okay," I yawned, giving in.

I didn't want to do this all alone if I didn't have to. I knew that no matter how prepared I thought I was, I didn't want to do this all without someone by my side. I knew I'd doubt my actions more than once.

I may also want my husband by my side every step of the way, but that was not an option, nor would it ever be. So, Taylor could be there if he wanted. I wouldn't fight him.

"How about some ice cream?" he asked, bringing me out of my depressed thoughts.

"Sure," I laughed, already liking the idea of something cold to eat. "As long as we do it after every appointment."

"Deal," he laughed.

I'd be okay. I had to be to prove to myself that I could do this.

This was now my life that I was stepping into with both feet. No turning back.

## Chapter 9

### Avidya

*Dear Diary,*

*It has been a few weeks. I know. But not writing has given me time to figure things out, at least somewhat. As much as I can for the time being. I still don't know if I'm doing the right thing, but I guess I'll find out in time.*

*In the past few weeks, it feels like I am doing the right thing. It may be the only thing that counts, but as long as it keeps me living, then I'll take it.*

*Three weeks ago, I left my husband. The one true person that I knew without a doubt that could keep me safe, give me what I've always wanted—love and peace—and I broke his heart to do so. I broke my own to do so.*

*I wonder if I made the right choice. I will always wonder. Now or ten years down the road. I will wonder if all this heartache was worth the price.*

*I know without a doubt that it will be.*

*My heart hurts and will continue to do so until I have the strength to face Zach again. I'm not sure I ever will. I fear what will happen when, and if, I ever do face him again.*

*I'm sure he has to hate me. I hate me.*

*I ran and haven't looked back. I can't. Not when I have life inside of me. I knew what would happen if I stayed. I would be devastated because I'd have been forced to do something I can't do.*

*I possibly can't see the good in choices if they are taken away from me.*

*Zach once promised me that he would never take my choices away. But he did. He was so angry at the thought of what could happen, that he took the choice clear away without a second thought. He promised me from the start that I would have a say over everything, but apparently not this thing that I was facing now.*

*I'm writing again. Not because my husband wanted me to while I lived with him, but so he can maybe someday understand my side of things. So he can understand why I ran. He has the right to know. It's the only thing I can possibly give him in return for the heartache I have caused him.*

*I can't write to him. I can't because I know I'll pour every little thing out to him if I sat down to do so. I have so much to say to him, yet nothing at all. I hurt so much, I don't know if anything can ever fix it. Instead, after I fill in each of these notebooks with my words, with my thoughts,*

*I'll send them to Carlos. He will be able to get them to my husband when he feels the time is right.*

*Why did I run? I'm sure he wants to know. Everyone I left wants to know. The answer can't be said yet. I can't trust him to know what I hold deeply in my heart. I know it's only a matter of time before he finds out from his father and even grandfather. But I can't give up the last living thing I have.*

*It's the reason I ran so far away. It's the reason I asked the man that first proposed to get me out of the life that I was no doubt destined for in one way or another.*

*I may be alone, for the most part, but I will be happy with my choices. I have to be.*

*If running broke my marriage, I can't ever be displeased with Zach's choices in life. Just as he can't with mine.*

*I'm tired, hurt, and happy all at once. I can envision my future and Zach isn't there. I can't see him here with me anytime soon. And that hurts. More than anything else.*

*I wish he could be. It'd make this easier. I wish I could be with my family. But, I can't.*

*I'm here. And there is nothing that can change now.*

*I'll be okay. I just hope that what I left behind will be okay too. I'm sorry for all the hurt that I have caused my departure. To everyone.*

    *But we all must move on.*

    *~Avidya*

Closing the new notebook I had gotten at the store just the day before, I set it on the little side table beside the bed. I had gotten in the habit to write a few times a week, and now that I was able to get a new notebook and pen, I figured I might as well start it back up. I needed some form of outlet, and this was one of the few things I could come up with.

Writing not only helped sort my thoughts out, but helped me get things written out that I couldn't say with spoken words. It helped to an extent, at least.

I also had picked up some new clothes, since I hardly brought anything with me. The weather was warmer, too, so I really needed shorts. I actually enjoyed shopping for myself for once. It hadn't happened all that often my entire life, so I certainly took advantage of it.

California weather was way too warm for being this close to winter. During the day, it was hot and humid. By the time the sun set, it was cold. I never wanted to go home as much as I did now. I'd love nothing but to be held against Zach's chest and hear his heartbeat within his chest.

Instead, I sat here on my borrowed bed, not sure what to do. I had yet to find a job, but I also hadn't been looking all that hard to find one, either. I really was just content to stay here and sleep my days away.

Taylor was welcoming, at least. He'd been busy working, but he tried to be there if I needed anything. Despite the first impressions I got from him, he did care about people. He was afraid to make friends, but who wouldn't be? One could never guess if someone would come up out of nowhere to find either of us.

The little picture that the doctor had printed off now sat on the nightstand in a simple green metal frame. It was too early to tell what the gender was, but I loved the baby nonetheless. I didn't care what it was. A boy. A girl. I'd love it no matter what.

I really was pregnant. I couldn't believe I was ten weeks today. It's crazy how fast times goes by.

Christmas was just a little over a month ago, and I'm still here. I'm surprised that Zachariah hadn't found me, dragging me back to where our home was. But first, he'd drag me to get rid of the baby, and I couldn't ever let that happen. I knew it was a matter of time. Only a matter of time before he showed up to do just that.

I just hoped that he would be a bit more willing to

see things from my view when the time came. I *prayed* that he would. After all, it was the only thing I could do right now.

Sighing, I flipped my legs over the edge of the bed and stood. Taylor was at work, the house was clean, and I was bored. Reading on my e-reader didn't sound all that appealing, either.

Maybe I did need a job to pass the time. Just not sure what. Taylor had no internet access, and for good reasons. I'd have been tempted to look up information on Zach if I was able to most likely.

Opening the door, I stepped outside. There was hardly anyone around at this time of day. Well, anytime, really. It was a quiet part of the neighborhood.

The thought of taking a walk was a possibility, if I wasn't afraid I'd get lost or be found by someone that didn't need to know who I was.

Leaving the screen door open, I took a seat on the steps, my hands hanging between my legs as I stared off to the horizon. Or what I could see of it. A small breeze caused my hair to slightly move. I could feel the incoming cold front that would be hitting us during the night that promised to bring rain.

I wondered what it would be like to live here, caring

for the baby. I had no idea what it would all entail, but I did need to find out so I could be prepared. Was there any way to be prepared?

What did I even need? And when did I need to start looking? There seemed to be so much to do, yet nothing to do at the same time.

"Hello!" greeted a little girl as she bounced her way over to me, stopping just feet before me. She could only be five years old or so. She wore a pale yellow dress, her hand playing at the bottom of it. Her dark red hair was pulled into pigtails, showing off her gray eyes as she took me in.

"Uh, hi," I said, giving her a smile.

"Catrina," called a lady, who I assumed was the child's mother. She looked a lot like the little girl, but a bit darker eyes and a few freckles along her cheekbones. "So sorry."

"It's okay," I shrugged. "I like kids."

"She likes everyone," she laughed. "I'm Krissy, by the way."

"Avidya," I replied.

"I haven't seen you around here before," Krissy mused, placing her hands on her daughter's shoulders.

"I just got here not long ago," I said. I hadn't hardly stepped foot out of the house until just this week, so of course she wouldn't have seen me here since I arrived.

"I didn't know that Mr. Shantez had any family," she hinted.

"He doesn't have much," I laughed, running a hand over my bare arm. Glimpsing the fading mark that had been left on my upper arm, a pang of hurt hit me. I brushed it off. "I'm his niece."

"Oh, that's nice," Krissy said. "He always seems so lonely. Glad he has family then. How long do you plan to stay?"

"For a while," I answered. "I was in between places and he offered me a room for as long as I need."

"If you need anything, I'd be happy to help," Krissy stated.

"Know of anyone hiring?" I asked jokingly.

"I do!" she said, her stormy gray eyes lighting up. "My friend runs as in-home daycare. She could use an extra pair of hands. Three days a week."

"Really? That'd be perfect," I said. "I used to work with kids at Sunday School."

"Do you have a phone?" she asked.

"A really old one," I laughed, holding up the flip phone that I had stuffed into my pocket. It was a burner phone, but worked to get ahold of Taylor if needed.

It would have been so easy to call Zachariah, to hear his voice. But I couldn't. I have no idea what would happen if I heard his voice. What could I even say to him if I called? A simple *sorry* was not going to work. I owed him more than just a few easy words.

She laughed, but didn't' say anything as she took the phone from my hand. As she handed it back, she spoke. "I entered my number, and my friend's—Bentley. Give her a call and she can work on getting you in there as soon as you'd like."

"Thanks," I said, grateful she was willing to help me in any way she could.

"Bentley is super nice!" Catrina gushed. "She watches me and like twenty other kids!" She held up both hands, showing me her version of how many twenty was.

She was adorable. I couldn't help but smile at her, letting my emotions show through my eyes.

"Only between five and eight, depending on the day," Krissy laughed. "My monkey over exaggerates. Constantly."

I couldn't help but smile at the girl. "Don't most?"

"Well, I better go. It was nice to meet you," Krissy said.

"You, too," I replied.

"Bye!" Catrina called as her mother took her by the arm.

"Bye," I said, giving her a wave.

"We should get together sometime. I'd hate to see you be all on your own like that uncle of yours," Krissy called over her shoulder as she was halfway to the house next door.

"Sure," I smiled. "I could use a friend or two here."

"Great!" Krissy smiled before continuing on her way.

Surely making a friend or two here wouldn't hurt me. There was no way I could let them know who I was, or that I was married to a mobster. But having someone to talk to sounded like a wonderful idea.

Maybe Karma was trying to show me that everything would be okay here.

## Chapter 10

## Zachariah

Another week went by. One day bled into the next, blurring into one extremely long day with very little sleep. But life goes on. Or so I tried to tell myself. Thanksgiving passed with me being held up here at the house. I couldn't face the family. I couldn't sit and try to be happy while my life slipped away from me.

I lived the best I could with this gaping hole in my chest. It felt like my soul had been taken away from me by the devil himself. I did what was expected. I kept my club running to top notch, bringing in a few new members here and there. I had to compensate for the loss of my brothel. It was officially closed down.

To worry about the safety of the girls and the men taking things too far was no longer a concern. I just didn't know what to do with my time now. I hoped that Avidya would be happy that the place was no longer. She didn't have good memories of that place, so I couldn't feel bad about it.

I'd do anything for her to come back, though. Anything at all. Didn't she know that?

Why hadn't she returned to me yet? Was she okay? *Where* was she?

I wanted another drink. Badly. My house was empty, lonely, and cold. How could I possibly live like this, feeling dejected? My parents, heck even Melio, constantly searched the house for any alcohol. It wouldn't have been that hard to buy and stash it somewhere, but then my father would have beat my ass again if I even tried.

They feared I'd just drink until I killed myself. Although that was an extremely tempting thought, I hadn't done it yet. I'm sure they realized that I could easily take my life by other means if I so wanted.

I wasn't suicidal. If my wife was no longer alive, that would be an entirely different story. I'd certainly have no reason to keep living if Avidya wasn't alive. It was bad enough that she wasn't with me now!

Since the club was closed during the daylight hours, for the most part, I was now left to my own thoughts once again. It wasn't a wise choice, but one I wanted all the same. I hated having to pretend to be interested in the club when I was there. At the same time, I hated being alone with my own consuming thoughts.

There was no in between.

I had no clue how everyone expected me to keep on

living. Could I do just that?

"Moping again?" Travis asked, foregoing knocking. Again.

"Go away," I grumbled, glaring at the man. Couldn't my family see I just wanted to be left alone in my own miserable thoughts?

"You know I can't do that," he stated, taking a seat in one of the chairs. "And you aren't the only one being affected by Avidya's disappearance."

I didn't remove my heated gaze from him. He was stepping on my toes, figuratively speaking of course. If I could get away with it, I'd have dragged him out of my house and locked the door behind him after making sure he'd never enter again.

"It's not only you that feels dejected and wronged. You aren't the only one that wants to know her reasons. We all do, Zach. But your father is right. What do you want her to come back to? To an empty shell who can't function, or to a man that knows how to survive by any means necessary?"

"It's not that simple," I grunted. It wasn't. But how much I wished it was.

I looked at Travis, seeing he didn't appear to be bothered nearly as bad as it was bothering me. Why couldn't he feel so lost as I was? Why did I have to hold on the brunt of all this anger?

I needed something to take away the pain. Every day that passed, I craved something more than just my dulled emotions to take the edge off of what I was feeling.

"You know something," my voice was hard as the words passed through my lips. The way he held himself, I knew he was holding something back from me.

"What do you mean?" he asked, seeming confused as I change the subject. His eyes spoke of the secrets he was hiding from me.

"You know something that concerns my wife," I gritted out. "What. Is. It?"

"I know as much as you do," he said slowly.

*Lie.*

"I swear. If I knew where she was, I'd bring her back myself," he stated, shifting in his seat. "I'd do just about anything to make her see reason, and see that leaving you was wrong. We are all suffering from her little disappearance."

"Do you know why she left?" I gritted through clenched teeth.

"Possibly, but not entirely sure," he said, leaning forward. "Remember what you may have said that made her upset. That'll give you a clue to why she ran."

He made absolute no sense.

"There was no way in hell she'd run because of my beliefs," I seethed. "Did she talk to you before she left? Did she say anything?" The words were nearly on top of each other as I spit out the questions.

Why hadn't I thought to question him before now?

"I wish she would have," Travis said sadly, leaning back in the chair. "Someone needs to talk some sense into her. Anyhow, think about why she may have wanted to run. Something happened, you just have to backtrack, and it should come to you."

"Why can't you just fucking tell me!" I snapped.

"It's not my secret to tell. You're gonna hate it, more than you hate the idea of her leaving, I'm sure," he shrugged, sitting back up fully.

He was no help. I shouldn't even have let his ideas cross my mind.

Was Travis trying to protect my wife, because she wanted it? Did he really not know where she was at?

Why wouldn't anyone just tell me where the fuck she was?

"Leave before I shoot you," I seethed at the man.

I was filled with such anger, I knew that if I had a

gun in my hands, I'd do just that. I'd shoot him. Because I could, and would.

Wisely, he did leave with giving me a concerned filled look.

Maybe I should just kill myself now and get this shit storm over and down with.

## Chapter 11

### Avidya

It was the day before Christmas, and one of the days I wasn't working. It had been easy to get in contact with Bentley, who turned out to be a wonderful friend and co-worker. Krissy and Bentley, and even their children, quickly became good friends. They both welcomed me in with open arms without any questions.

It was strange to be welcomed so warmly. So quickly. I didn't know what I was expecting, but it wasn't that. I never had friends growing up outside of Becca, so everything was so different outside of the hold my parents had over me.

So much was so freaking different in a matter of months.

All that I was willing to give up was that I was pregnant, because there was no way I'd be able to keep that secret for much longer, and that I had left the baby father due to bad circumstances. I never discussed who he was, nor what he did. My new friends didn't pry, either.

They supported me in my choice and they were there for me when things got a bit overwhelming emotionally.

Some days were worse than others. Some days I was so drawn down, I didn't want to get out of bed. Other days, I was able to push all thoughts out of my head to keep on living. Knowing my choices made a difference to the baby I carried helped me get up each morning.

Having a support team behind me made a huge difference. One that I couldn't be happier to have, even if I was grumpy most days because I missed having my husband by my side. It was my choice, and I kept my mouth shut about it.

Taylor was a constant presence, which helped more than he'd ever know. He was able to get off work to take me to each doctor appointment, where everything was looking great. I was now just shy of seventeen weeks, and slightly showing if I wore a tight shirt.

Thankfully, the nausea had passed, and I wasn't nearly as tired constantly. Don't get me wrong, I was still tired by the end of the day and crashed shortly after dinner almost every night.

Everything was going as well as I could expect. I had people who were there for me, a place to live, and a job. I didn't think anything worse could happen now that things were starting to look up finally. I had talked Taylor into going to church at least once a month with me. He wasn't thrilled, but he did anyhow without too much complaint.

I went to church every Sunday, hoping that it'd help get me out of my depression that I knew I suffered with. It was all my fault, and I had to change things so I could live. I couldn't let all my hard work go to waste.

Church helped more than friends and family, truthfully. I knew God put these people in my path that I had met so far for a reason, along with giving me a baby that I would no doubt love forever. Most of all, I knew that God's love would be what helped get me through life, no matter how hard it would get through the next however many years I would have.

The day before Christmas, I slept as late as I could before starting my day. Being in California, it was strange that it didn't feel like the holidays. It was too warm, and not cold.

I wasn't sure what I was going to do all day, but I felt happy, like things were finally looking up. I had been expecting Zachariah, or even one of his guards, to come find me. But there had been no one. Not a squeak or peep out of anyone that may be looking for me. Not even Aaron.

I still wasn't entirely sure what he wanted out of

me, but as long as he didn't find me again, I'd be perfectly fine.

The ringing of my cell phone caused me to jump slightly, bringing me out of my thoughts. Glancing at the number, I saw it was only Carlos calling. He had made sure to call me every few days, just to check in. I wasn't sure why, but I never questioned it. Maybe he was just concerned that I wasn't happy.

With a shrug, I answered the phone with a simple "Hello."

"Avidya," Julia's name came through the speaker with a sigh of relief.

"Uh, hi," I said, loss of words. No one but Carlos had called, well, other than the people who I knew here.

"Carlos is going to hate me, but I had to talk to you. How are you, dear?" she said quickly.

Did she steal her husband's phone to call me? I knew they were pretty open about sharing their phones if they ever needed to, but why would she willing call me? Didn't she hate me for leaving?

"Doing okay," I answered.

"I miss you," Julia sighed out. "We all do."

"I miss you all too," I replied, forcing my tears to stay at bay.

"Please, come back home, Avidya," she said, near tears herself.

"I can't," I shook my head, even though she couldn't see it. "I'm sorry. I can't come back."

"Why not?" she asked, sniffing.

"I just can't," I sighed. "I'm sorry. I really am. I just can't come back. I had to leave."

"You're pregnant, aren't you?" she asked knowingly.

For once, her assumption was right on. I kept quiet, not able to answer her. I feared if I did, she'd somehow talk me into going back home. I desperately wanted to. I just couldn't. Not yet.

"How far along?" she asked, her voice quiet.

"Almost seventeen weeks now," I whispered out. "You can't tell anyone."

"I won't. I promise," she said quickly. "When will you come back? Toby hasn't been doing well either."

"I don't know," I said, taking a seat at the table. I knew that Toby would be affected, that was a given. Everyone was. "I don't know if I ever will."

"Okay," Julia sighed, knowing there was no use in trying to get me to change my mind. "Where are you?"

"Somewhere," I shrugged out. "I will come back

when I am ready."

"You're safe, right?" she quickly asked.

"Yes," I said, not having to think about it. "I have everything I need here."

"That's good," she said, sounding like she was relieved. "Can I call you again?"

"Sure," I said after a moment. I think I could handle talking to her more often. I missed everyone so much.

"Great," she said, a smile in her voice. "Please, give Zach a call. It'd help him cool his temper some. I swear, that man thinks the world revolves around him."

I couldn't help but let a laugh out at that. It was a sad heartbroken one, but a laugh all the same.

"It'd make him feel better to know you are, in fact, okay," Julia said. "Please. It's the least you could do."

"I'll think about it," I sighed out. I wanted to hear his voice, badly. Was it worth more pain? Would it solve anything?

"Thank you," Julia said before hanging up. There was no good bye.

As I closed the phone, I let the tear fall. I missed them all so freaking much. More than anything else in the world.

But I had to keep on going.

## Chapter 12

### Zachariah

Monsters were my only friends now. My family, I had to give them credit, tried to make things better. But it was all a lost cause. There was nothing that could make me feel better. Nothing but my wife.

Since I refused to partake in the holiday, everyone came to me instead. I hated it. Why couldn't they just let me do what I wanted for once? Why couldn't they just let me stay home and wallow in my misery alone?

It felt like everyone was determined to make me see the light, whatever good that would do. The light had been gone for a while now.

With my family here, I sat in my office, wallowing alone as much as I could. Their voices reached me every so often. I did everything I could to block them out.

I couldn't help but wonder what it'd be like if Avidya was here. She'd have loved to be a part of all this. She'd maybe even have decorated the house, making it feel more like the holiday spirit. It certainly would make the house feel more like a house than a prison.

As the days passed, the house grew colder and

lonelier. I had been spending as much time as I possibly could outside of the house. It didn't matter what I was doing, as long as I didn't have be here. Today was one of the very few days I had no option be stuck inside. I would have done anything to get out, but I knew if I tried, someone would stop me.

"How about you come join us?" Grandma said as she stood in the doorway. She gave me that look that said she'd bring the Don into it if she had too. My grandmother may look tiny, but her words were quite powerful when needed. Her and grandpa really were the perfect match; both strong-willed people who butted heads as often as they got along, but still wonderful together.

"Fine," I sighed out. I stood while pinching my nose. Might as well get this over and done with. The sooner it was over, the quicker I could try to find something to take away my pain again. Not that anything was helping so far.

"She's better off without you," Grandma huffed, walking away.

"Just say what you want to say, why don't you," I muttered back with a bite to my tone.

"See, that is why. That girl doesn't deserve you. You can't even live without her," she stated with a shake of her head. "I'd have run off too. If I didn't want to die, I would have a number of times."

Wisely, I kept my mouth shut. I didn't want to start something I shouldn't. Not with this woman. She wasn't scared of slapping me around to get her point across to me if needed.

With heavy steps, I entered the living room, looking around at all the family members. Violet was trying to get Toby to talk, or at least do something other than sit on the sofa with his knees pulled to his chest as he stared off into space. Toby had grown a lot in the past few months with a good healthy diet, I noticed. Melio was joking around with Travis, who had been welcomed into this family way too easily the last few weeks. My father and grandfather were in a heated discussion about something that I didn't want to hear at the moment.

"About time you joined us," Melio said as I took a seat on the far end of the couch that the boy was sitting on.

"If I could have gotten away with it, I wouldn't have," I muttered, slouching in the seat.

"What happened to that strong, powerful man you once were? Surely a girl can't cause that much damage," Keena stated. A statement from a Domme who knew what she wanted out of life didn't sit well with me.

"Life. Life happened," I said.

I wasn't as strong any more. It was hard to be someone I wasn't while in front of my family. I was torn down into nothing. Why would I need to pretend for my family now? Who cared what I was anymore?

"I want Vidie!" Toby's loud voice rose above everyone else's that was in the room. It felt like all noise instantly stopped as he talked.

"I know you do, sweetie. But she's not here. There's no need to yell, either," Violet was quick to try to soothe him.

I knew how the kid felt. I wanted her too.

"She has to come back!" he said, his voice filled with despair. His dark eyes pinned me in my place. "You made her leave! I don't like you. It's all your fault!"

"I didn't do anything," I huffed out, leaning my head back against the back of the couch. "She can come back anytime she fucking wants to."

"Toby, she wanted to leave," Julia said, kneeling down in front of him. "She misses you, though."

"How'd you know that? It's not like she will ever talk to any of us," he huffed with labored breathing.

"I talked to her yesterday. She'll come back when she's ready," my mom said quietly.

At her words, I popped my eyes opened. She talked to my wife? How?

"But he made her leave. He didn't want her! She left me. She promised she wouldn't. I want her to come back," he cried out.

"We all do," Mom said. "And she will when she feels it's safe here."

"She said it was safe here," Toby breathed out. "I want her."

Before anyone could react, Toby launched himself off the couch and ran up the stairs. No one chased him. No one tried to get him to come back.

Why couldn't they do that to me? Why couldn't they just let me go and run off my pent-up frustration?

"When did you talk to her?" Carlos asked. He didn't seem all that surprised, but he wasn't happy, either.

"Yesterday," Mom answered, standing up and wiping away non-existent wrinkles from her dress pants.

"Figured you'd have called sooner," Carlos said with a shrug. "Get what you wanted?"

"No," Mom said with a sad smile. Turning to me she said, "Make sure you answer your phone today."

"Why?" I asked.

"Just do," was all she said before saying something

about checking on dinner.

~oOo~

It was just after eleven that night when everyone finally left. The house was once against dark, cold, and empty. Toby had been hiding in the spare bedroom, refusing to come out until Avidya came home. Poor kid. I wish I could have hidden until she came back home, too. But I was a grown man and that just wasn't acceptable to act like a child.

I was tired and ready for bed, but I knew sleep would not be coming to me willingly once more. I was lucky if I got a couple hours of sleep each night. Most nights, I laid awake thinking. I had taken to sleeping on the couch or in the office. I hadn't looked twice at the bed. I physically couldn't.

I couldn't help but wonder what had happened to me. I used to be tough and everyone would easily cower in fear from me. Now, I was a snobby, depressed man. How could one simple girl change me so much?

It didn't make sense. I had to find that tough man again. I had to be strong. No more moping. At least not around people. I could hide my true feelings from the family. I'd done it before.

The ringing of the house phone rang through the house. I debated answering it, since no one ever called that phone. As it rang the fourth time, I took a deep breath and answered.

"Hello?" my voice was rough, filled with lack of sleep and patience.

I could hear breathing, but no one spoke for what felt like years.

"If you aren't going to talk, I'll just hang up," I muttered down the line.

"Please, don't," Avidya's voice came through. Her voice was quiet, soft, and just as I remembered.

"Alright," I sighed, running a hand down my face. I had no idea what to say to her. There was so much, yet nothing I could say. After a few seconds of nothing coming from either of us, I finally took a breath and said something. "I miss you. So fucking much."

"I miss you, too," she spoke. She sounded tired, just as tired as me if it was possible. "How...How are you?"

"Fucked up," I said. I wasn't going to pretend for her. Anyone but her. "I want you back, Avidya. Please."

I would fucking beg for this woman to come back to

me. Right this minute.

“I…I’m sorry,” she said with a tear-filled voice.

My shoulders slumped. “Why?”

“You’ll hate me. I can’t face you right now. You…I’m sorry,” she spoke.

“I can’t hate you. Never,” I said. “I love you more than life itself.”

“But you will when know my reasons,” she sighed.

“Tell me, then. Tell me them so I can figure out how to make this all right,” I asked, nearly begging already.

“You can’t,” she said sadly. “This is all on me. There is nothing you can do, Zach.”

“I miss you. Please, would you just come back? I’ll make it all better. I’m so sorry for whatever I did,” I said. I had to fix whatever I did to make her leave me. I wish I knew what I did so I could fix is now.

“You didn’t do anything, Zach,” she said. “I’ll come back when I know it’s safe. I can’t…I’m…” she trailed off. I could hear her softly crying on the other end.

“Please,” I whispered. I wanted to reach through the phone and pull her back home. Pull her into my arms to hold her tightly and never ever let her go again. “When will you come back? Toby misses you, too.”

Maybe if she knew Toby was just as upset as the

rest of them, she'd return. Maybe she'd come back for one of us.

"You have no idea how much I miss him. I miss you so much," she said, clearing her throat. "But I can't."

"Why the fuck not?" I shouted. I heard her intake of breath, but it didn't stop me. "Why can't you fucking come back and deal with this like an adult?"

"When you can act like one, I will," she spoke, her voice soft and smooth. "I'll come back when I know you won't act stupid about the choices I've made. I bet you haven't even figured out why I ran, have you?"

"No," I grunted out. "No one will tell me a fucking thing."

I was happy to hear her voice, but I wanted to hold her. I wanted to see her. I just wanted her back home. Why couldn't she be back home.

"That's for the best," she said quietly.

"I'll come track you down and drag you back here," I seethed.

I wanted to punch something. Anything.

"I'm surprised you haven't yet," she stated. Was that what she was waiting for? Was she wanting me to track her down to drag her back home? Because I wanted to. I hadn't yet because I had no clues to finding her or I would have already.

"I will if you don't tell me why you ran," I threatened.

"You haven't yet, therefore you still won't," she said, almost amused. "Who knows, maybe one day I'll just show up on your doorstep with my reason for running."

"Please do. Like right now," I gritted out.

"Or maybe one day, I'll get back to the place I'm staying, and you'll just be sitting here, waiting for me. A look of pure fury on your face," she mused.

"Avidya, please," I said. Was she playing with me? "Would you come back with me, if I did show up?"

"As long as you grow up, yes. I can't give up my own beliefs for you. Not when someone else is involved," she answered.

"What do you mean by that?" I asked.

"Just think about it. I'm sure it'll come to you. If not, when you ever get the balls to grow up, please come find me. I don't want this anger-filled man on my doorstep. I want the man that I fell in love with. The man that took control, but let me have complete say over everything I want. I want the man that will hold my wishes and my broken heart in his hands. I want that man to come find me and put us back together.

"I may have left, but you have ways to find me. Think about it. Think about what you could really do. Prove to yourself that you deserve me. Because right now, I don't think you do. Not when you took that one choice away from me. It could have been any choice, but it had to be the one I knew I'd never be able to look past." She paused for a moment, gathering her thoughts.

"It's late. I love you, Zachariah." With that, she hung up, not giving me a chance to reply.

What the fuck just happened? She made no sense to me, and now I was more confused than I had been the day she left me.

## Chapter 13

## Avidya

Days turned into weeks. Weeks turned into months. Time passed, and I kept on going through each passing minute as well as I could. I didn't worry about the possibilities. I didn't worry about what could happen later on in my life. I only worried about the here and now. There was no point in worrying about things I no longer had control over.

It was after the new year and I hoped that with it came good things. I prayed that things would work out on their own. I was done with worrying over everything, at least as much as I could.

I had been filled with nerves when I called Zach on Christmas, I wasn't even sure he'd answer. I called late at night for a reason. I halfway hoped that he wasn't going to answer, so I could just leave a message. But when he answered, I had wanted to say so many things. I wanted to tell him my secret. I wanted him to come find me.

I had told him to come find me. I basically dared him to. I was surprised he hadn't yet. I think, since it had been almost five months since I left him, it gave him enough time to cool down. When I talked to him, I could hear in his voice that he hated life. He hated me leaving. And he hated himself.

So I told him to grow up, but maybe not in a nice way. He needed to grow up. He needed to take charge and come get me, damn it. Because I knew if he did, I wouldn't fight him. I would go with him willingly. I wanted to see him so badly, I would have done so without second thought.

I had enough people on my side to make sure that the baby would be mine, no matter what. Maybe if I had given them all time before now, they would be on my side no matter what. With my time away, I found that having time on my own was needed. Needed for me to figure out my life. It helped me more than I ever thought it would.

As the days passed, I kept busy with working at the daycare and keeping an eye on Catrina when Krissy had to work late a few nights a month. I didn't mind at all. I enjoyed it.

Taylor and I got along well, and I had told him that I wished he'd have gotten me as a kid instead of where I ended up. He had looked dumbfounded, then grunted something about not being sure what I was talking about.

He didn't take compliments very well. Neither did I

most days.

We were more alike than either one of us had ever thought.

Today, since I wasn't needed at the daycare, I sat in the bedroom. I was thinking about how to fit a small crib in here, because there were only a few months left before the baby would be arriving. Later today, I'd be finding out the gender, and I was excited. I couldn't wait to know what I was having.

It seemed like it wasn't all that long ago when I felt its first kicks from inside of me. I cherished each moment I got with this little one. Taylor was a bit freaked out at the fact that I had forcibly laid his hand on my growing stomach to feel that first night I felt the kicks. His look was filled with disgust before turning to awe, which he had quickly tried to hide.

I didn't plan to buy much, since I wasn't sure when Zach would show up. But I wanted to buy a few things here and there. Every time I went to the store, I always had to stop and look at all the cute little baby items. It was so tempting to buy things already. Well, I had bought a few soft gender-neutral blankets that were soft and fuzzy.

So far, I refused to think of what I was going to name the baby. I wanted Zach to help, even if he didn't want to. Only time would tell. And I had more than enough time to wait and waste away.

"Hey, Vids," Taylor said, popping his head around the corner.

"Uh, hey. Shouldn't you be at work?" I asked, turning to face him.

"A short day," he shrugged. I wasn't sure I believed him, as he worked at some construction site as a security guard.

"Shorter than normal," I stated.

"Well," he trailed off, not sure what to say. "I may have asked to get off early. I wanted to get you something."

"You didn't need to do that," I said. What could he have possibly gotten me?

"I wanted to," he said. "It's in the living room."

Giving him a questioning look, I got up from the bed and made my way to the living room. There, I found a boxed bassinet with a number of bags on the top.

"What? When?" I asked, not able to tear my eyes away from it.

"Today," he said sheepishly. "I know you need it, and I wasn't sure if you'd ever go get it yourself. So yeah. I just got it. I hope that's okay." He ran a hand across his hair, trying to hide his nerves.

"Thank you," I said, flinging my arms around him in a hug. I didn't know how else to thank him, even though he wasn't that much of a touchy-feely person.

He returned the hug awkwardly.

"I'll help put it together and all that," he said once I released him. "It should fit in the room without a problem. There's blankets and other stuff you'll need, too."

"Thank you. You really didn't need to, you know," I said as I started to look through the bags.

"I wanted to. I can spoil my family how I want to," he grunted before heading to the kitchen.

I let him be as I sorted through the bags. There were soft fleece blankets, receiving blankets, and some cute little socks. Even a matching hat. It was all adorable and I couldn't wait to use them.

"I was going to wait till after your appointment, but figured it wouldn't hurt to get the stuff now," Taylor said, taking a seat at the table with a cup of coffee.

"I love it. Thank you," I smiled his way. My hair fell over my shoulder as I sat one of the bags onto the floor.

"Don't forget you'll have to call Julia and Carlos after the appointment," Taylor reminded me.

"I'm sure one of them will be calling before I ever get done," I laughed.

"Possibly," he agreed with an amused laugh.

Julia had made sure to give me a call almost weekly, beating her husband to it most of the time. I didn't mind. It was nice to be able to talk to her. It felt like I needed that connection more than I had realized. She kept me up to date on most of the things that she could throughout the weeks. So far, it didn't seem like Zach was looking for me. I wasn't sure if he was just trying to keep it all quiet, or if he was just planning for the right moment.

Whatever he was doing, I was waiting for him.

~oOo~

I lay on the table, the cold gel smeared across my stomach. I think Taylor was more nervous than I was currently. He sat stiffly in the chair beside me, hands clasped too tightly in his lap.

"You are finding out the gender, correct?" the tech asked as she grabbed the wand to look inside of my belly.

"Yes," I answered, watching on the screen above as she used the wand to begin to take measurements.

"Perfect," she smiled. "Hopefully the little one will corporate so we can get a good look. So far, everything looks like it's developing perfectly. On the small side, but not so much that it's anything to be concerned about."

She took measurements of everything that had to do with the baby. She walked me through what each part was, not at all concerned about any of it.

"Alright," she said. "It looks like it's a boy!"

"A boy?" Taylor gulped. "You sure?"

"Positive," she smiled. "I have some pictures being printed off for you to keep, and if there are any concerns, your doctor will call you within twenty-four hours. But I see no reason to worry."

"Thank you," I said as I cleared away the goop that covered my rounding belly with the oversized hand towel that she handed me.

"Of course," she smiled.

It hadn't taken long to get changed and cleaned up before heading back to the truck. Of course, we stopped for ice cream, as per usual.

I was having a baby boy. I had no idea what Zach would do once he found out, but I'd do anything in my power to make sure that this baby was loved as much as possible.

## Chapter 14

### Zachariah

Before I knew it, spring was upon us. The rain turned into spring showers, the birds began to chirp, and everything was born anew. Only if my heart would be too.

After the phone call from Avidya on Christmas night, I finally *grew a pair*, as everyone kept telling me. I became the hard man I was known to be among my men and others that knew me. I was feared. A feared monster.

I ran my club, making sure everything was going smoothly. I ordered new equipment with the plans to expand to increase the member count. It all brought in more money, which was the main reason in doing everything I was.

Both of my parents seemed to be happy. Apparently, Avidya called them a number of times the past few weeks. Mom said she's doing well, and hopefully would return home sooner rather later. God, I hoped so.

I didn't hold too much hope on that. She hadn't called me again. I wished she would. I wanted to hear her voice. I wanted to know where she was at. I just wanted *her!* I had looked for the number that she called me from, but it was blocked, so I had no way of calling her myself. It didn't stop me from answering the phone every time it rang.

Currently, Travis was away looking for any leads on where she may be. He was the best man to track down anyone that didn't want to be found. He had mentioned that she may be closer than I thought to look. Did that mean he knew where she was? Was it possible that she was so close that I didn't even know it?

Jonas was my own personal bodyguard as I continued to dig up information on Aaron and his gang. I knew he wasn't working alone. I just had to figure out who was working on his side. There wasn't all that much digging to do, though, as the man was pretty much an open target. It just wasn't as fun and thrilling now that I didn't have to chase him down. I knew right where he was, but I was biding my time. He'd come to me soon enough.

Lynn had come crawling back a few weeks ago. She was upset her daughter wasn't here with me, and refused to listen to reason. I didn't know what to do about her, so I sent her away. What else was I supposed to do? Her daughter wasn't here, and I didn't know if Avidya would even want to see that woman.

Although she appeared calm on the surface, Lynn

was skittish like something would jump out and attack her at any given moment. She was tight-lipped about what made her that way, too. I could only gather she was afraid that Aaron was coming for her. Little did she know, that man wanted nothing to do with her. He only wanted what was mine.

I was able to talk her into just going home with a promise that I'd let her know if her daughter ever turned up. If she really cared, she'd do more than she had so far. Like actually try to be a parent. I was sure she knew I wasn't happy with her; it was pretty clear about that. When a mother gave up their child for their own sick pleasure, I didn't look on too kindly about the choices.

Sure, she may have done what she thought was right, but it would have just been better if she'd have gone to my father and ask for our protection instead of going behind everyone's back to do it.

Personally, I didn't care what happened to her. My wife hadn't really cared, either, as far as I knew. Avidya never asked for updates; never asked for me to look harder. Everything was just as it had been with no change.

The ringing of my phone jarred me from my thoughts, thankfully. More and more applications for people who wanted to join the club kept coming in, it was increasing weekly.

"Travis," I answered, rubbing my dry eyes at the same time as I leaned back in my chair. My lack of sleep was slowly catching up with me.

"I have some information," he answered easily. The sounds of cars were heard in the background.

"I'm listening," I answered.

"Avidya is in Cali," he said. "Living with a man named Taylor Shantez."

"Ah, the mystery of where that man has been is solved," I muttered, but happy for some good news.

"Yes," he said. "I can't get close, though. He won't be afraid to shoot me on sight if he sees me. I saw her leaving the house this afternoon, and she looks...well, happy."

"That's good," I said. I think. I wasn't sure if I wanted her to be happy. Why should she have to suffer, but why should she be happy, either?

Yeah, I know. I don't know what I wanted my wife to *be*. Alive, at least. Alive. That I could deal with.

"Can you talk to her? Bring her back?" I fired off.

"I will," he said. "She left with a red-haired chick and a kid. Not sure where they went since the redhead chick drove a car, and drove like a bat shit crazy lady."

"How long did it take for you to track her down?" I asked.

"Wasn't all that hard, really. I listened to small talk at the diner about a new girl in town that was sweet, and she was staying with the quietest man in town," he stated. "Only took me about a day to track what house she was staying in." He paused, thinking over something before continuing. "I'll catch her when she returns home. It's early enough, maybe she has a job or something."

"Keep me posted," I stated before hanging up.

I trusted Travis to talk to her. Maybe he could be the only one that could talk some sense into that crazy woman that I loved more than life itself. At least she was alive, safe, and healthy. It was all I could ask for at this point in time.

Oh, but when I would have her back here in my arms, she'd get punished. My palm ached to swat that round ass of hers until she begged me to stop.

Crap. I had to stop thinking like that. I was stressed, and I knew I needed some sort of release. But I was a man of my word.

I wouldn't harm her, but she'd fucking be sorry for leaving me.

## Chapter 15

### Avidya

After telling Krissy bye for the day and heading to my house, I couldn't help but let a smile form on my lips. Today had been a good day at work. No one threw up and the kids actually got along pretty well. Also, there was a new twelve-week-old, who was adorably cute and small.

Everything was going smoothly as far as I was concerned. I was only a short eight weeks from my due date and this past weekend we'd a small baby shower. Krissy was determined to have one for me, which I didn't fight her on.

Only thing missing was my entire family, but I was happy. I didn't have a huge gaping hole where my heart was now. Thinking about my past hurt, but it was bearable. Every day it was more bearable.

Opening the front door, I froze. My heart beat in my chest in heavy thumps. My eyes widened in horror. Fear consumed me. My stomach twisted into knots.

Time froze.

In the living room, tied to a chair and unconscious was Taylor. His head hung down to his chest, his breathing slow. Behind him stood a man that looked way too much like Cody, but a bit pudgier and shorter. His eyes were a tad lighter, but still, I could see the pain he wished to cause me.

I hadn't expected to come home to this. Anything but this. I had been so prepared to come home every day to find my husband waiting for me. Or even for any other family member to be waiting to take me back because something had happened to Zachariah.

Anything but this.

*Oh God. Where are you? Please, oh please, come now.*

"Well, don't just stand there, child. Come in. Shut the door, too," the man spoke in a demanding voice.

Slowly, I entered the house fully and shut the door behind me. I could have easily ran, but I didn't trust the man that had a gun pointed at my head. He could easily shoot me before I took a step outside.

"Good girl," he said, giving me a toothy smile. Most of his teeth were yellow from years of smoking and drugs no doubt.

I remained quiet. What did he want? How did he find me? Why was he here?

"Have a seat," he said, nodding to the couch.

"Can I go pee first?" I asked, not moving. "Or I'll

pee my pants."

"Fine. Make it quick," he grunted out.

I nodded, taking steps backward, not removing my eyes from him. I didn't trust this man. There was no way in hell I'd ever trust him. When I reached the bathroom, I shut the door and turned on the water slightly.

Oh, God. What was I going to do? Aaron was in my house. He was in the one place that I thought was safest from him. Safest from anyone that wanted to harm me. What did he want?

My breaths came fast and choppy. My heart beat in overtime. I forced myself to get my act together. I couldn't panic. Not yet. I could when this was all over with.

Being seven months pregnant, I couldn't afford to panic. I also couldn't afford to let things get too far carried away.

Leaning my hands on the countertop, I looked at myself in the mirror. I mentally told myself to get a freaking grip. I could get through this. I had to.

My stomach tightened, causing my breath to hitch for a moment before the pain passed.

With shaking hands, I pulled my phone from my purse and dialed the one number that I knew would no doubt be able to help. I knew I had to.

"Hello," Kent's voice came through on the first ring.

"He's here. Aaron is here," I whispered hurriedly.

"In the house?" Kent asked, fully alert.

"Yes," I whispered, my words filled with worry.

"Okay. Stay calm, okay," he said.

Stay calm? Really? I was passed that.

"Where are you?" he asked.

"Bathroom." My simple answer.

"Okay. I'll have someone there very soon. But I need you to listen, okay. You will walk back out there in in just a few minutes. Don't give away that you called me, or have any way of calling me. I'll be deactivating your phone after this call, so he can't try to use it against you. When you walk out there, don't say anything. Do whatever he wants. Just don't leave the house with him, okay. Stay inside. My men will be there in less than ten minutes."

"Okay," I breathed.

"You'll be okay," he said.

"He has a gun," I breathed out.

"So do you. Taylor has guns hidden throughout the house. Can you find one?"

"There's none in the bathroom."

"That's fine," Kent said easily as though it didn't

matter.

"Hurry up!" Aaron shouted out, causing me to jump.

"Go on," Kent said. "Put your phone in a pad or something, then go back out there. Just hang in there, Avidya."

He hung up, expecting me to do just that. Which I did, of course. I quickly stuffed the phone into a bag of pads that had gone unused. I had just turned off the water as the door swung open, an angry filled Aaron in the doorway.

"You done?" he asked.

I nodded my head, watching him in fear.

He moved his head to the side, indicating that I needed to go to the living room as he waited. Once there, I took a seat on the couch, my hands folded protectively around my stomach. I wished I had worn a shirt that didn't show off my baby bump today. With my arms folded over my baby, I felt him kick a few times, more than normal. The ache in my gut was still there. Not sharp, but annoyingly so.

"Is he okay?" I asked towards Taylor.

"He'll be fine," Aaron said. "But you are one hard gal to track down, did ya know that?"

I shrugged in answer.

"Let me tell ya this," he went on, swinging his gun around in the air. I couldn't help but grimace at his actions. Did he even know how to use that *thing* he had in his hand? "I wasn't sure what I want to do with ya. I knew that *woman* didn't do as I had told her to do. I knew what would happen if I ever had a spawn with my blood. I knew what fate would be laid out clear as day.

"I always made sure that I had no one to keep the blood of my family going. I am sure you know about how powerful it had once been. Everyone wants to blame me for not doing my part or not selling the drugs that I was meant to sell. Does it really matter, though?"

He paused, seeming to debate on something as Taylor grunted in his seat as he came back to the real world.

"So, what do you want with me, then?" I asked. After all this time, he had to want something.

"I had planned to just kill ya. I had someone that was meant to do that, but apparently, he was on the payroll of your so-called husband. Stupid of him, but I guess someone took him out before I could for failing at doing his job. Where is that husband, anyhow?" he asked, rubbing his chin with the butt of the gun.

I couldn't help but mentally laugh at how stupid he was. I may not know how to use a gun all that well, but I knew the basics. Never point it at yourself unless you intended to use to kill yourself.

"Not here," I said, my voice stronger than I expected as I said the words. "He didn't want me."

"Why? He was so intent on keeping you safe," he said, genuinely worried about that. He slowly pointed the gun at the floor. "His family is always here."

"Because they don't trust me to not blab my mouth," I lied. "I wasn't the girl he wanted after he found out I wouldn't bow to his wishes."

"Then who's kid?" he asked, glancing at my stomach.

"It's mine," Taylor said before I could answer. His voice was low and hoarse, but still powerful as he shifted in his seat.

"Huh," Aaron hummed. "Whatever floats your boat. I didn't know you liked to be an inbred fucktard." His voice darkened in disgust.

"Will you answer my question?" I asked softly, looking at the man in an almost pleading way.

"What should I do with ya?" Aaron asked. He began to pace. Did he even know what he wanted to do? He seemed so unsure of his own actions.

"He won't do shit," Taylor said. "Always a man of threats, but never fucking follows through. I know you all too well. It's always the same thing."

"Shut up," Aaron seethed towards Taylor.

"Or what?" Taylor laughed. "You've had the chance to kill me, and yet you haven't. I don't think you have the balls to do it. You want something."

"I want many things, *brother*," Aaron laughed. "None of which I will get."

"Maybe I can help," I spoke up, hoping to get the man to calm down. My heart beat too fast in my chest.

*Where were the men that Kent said he was sending? Shouldn't they be here by now?*

"I wanted a family, ya know," Aaron sighed out. "But that was so long ago. Now. Well, now, I want the Melendez family to pay for taking my family down. I want them to beg for your life, which they will never get in the end. Because I will control your life."

"Just like what Cody did? Are you that sick in the head?" Taylor said, clearly amused.

"I am nothing like that man!" Aaron shouted in rage.

"Then act like it!" Taylor returned just at hotly.

"So, what will you do?" I asked, hoping he'd just freaking answer me. I may have fear consuming me, but I had to keep him talking.

"I don't know," Aaron muttered out. He placed both hands on his head, the gun still in his right, as he pulled at his hair. "I don't know. I don't fucking know!"

"Are you okay?" Taylor asked me as Aaron paced the house, muttering to himself.

"He hasn't touched me," I whispered. I gathered that was what he wanted to know.

I wanted to know how long the man had been in our house, and how the heck he even got in. I knew Taylor wouldn't let this man into the house by any means.

"Good," Taylor said. Louder, he asked, "Can I have some water?"

"Get it," Aaron nodded my way as he peeked through the window.

Quickly, I got up and got a class of water for him. My hands were shaky as my eyes landed on the knife that sat on the countertop next to the chopping board. Glancing behind me, Aaron had returned to his pacing.

Praying that I didn't get either of us killed, I took ahold of the knife and cup of water, making my way back to Taylor. He gave me a knowing nod.

Purposely, I dropped the glass on the carpet, watching as it bounced and made a wet spot. At the same moment, another cramp bit through my lower body, causing me to huff out a painful breath.

"Shoot," I muttered, bending down behind Taylor to pick up the glass.

Aaron didn't notice, nor care. He seemed to be fighting with his thoughts on what to do. Were mental issues a common thing in this family? Was he insane?

Quickly and quietly, I used the knife to cut through the thin rope that forcibly kept Taylor's arms behind the chair before slipping the handle of the knife into his hand.

"You okay?" Taylor asked quietly.

"Fine," I whispered, knowing I wasn't.

"Did you make a call?" Aaron asked me harshly, causing me to freeze.

I shook my head, my eyes wide in fear.

Did someone finally come to save us? *Oh God, please.*

He didn't reply. Instead, he marched to the bathroom. I could hear the banging of doors as he looked in every little nook and cranny that could possibly hide a phone.

I met Taylor's eyes, and he looked way too calm.

Was this something he'd expected after all these years? Why was it always me that had to be forced into such situations?

"Then who would be here?" Aaron asked as he stormed out of the bathroom.

"No one," I answered slowly. "Please."

"What should I do? I can't just let you both live. I can't be found here. I can't die. I should. I've skipped that way too many times already. How can I get out of this?" he mumbled to himself. Finally, he met my eyes. Would he answer my question?

"I am sorry you were born. Ya know, if Racheal would have just did what I told her to do, you wouldn't have to suffer like this. I just didn't want any kids then, but now that I see how much you look like her, I think I've changed my mind. I didn't want to feel like this. I'm so fucking out of control.

"I didn't know you were alive until Cody called me, though. He needed money, and wanted to know how to get money, fast. He knew that you would be married off. It was just a matter of time, and to whom you'd be tied to for the rest of your life. He hated the fact that he had to have you, but it came with keeping his name protected.

"He was always a good actor; I'd give him that. But

he could only act for so long. Lynn, for whatever reason he married that slut, was a pain in his ass. And mine. She had gotten the Melendez family involved. I warned him, but he didn't consider what would happen if he kept it all up," he rushed to get everything out.

What did this all have to do with me?

"I told him I'd take you," Aaron laughed. "I told him I'd keep you safe. But I had other motives for that. But that was only to cover up my own needs. I could use you as a motive to get my money from the men that owed me. I wanted to use you as a way to prove that money would be nothing without a pretty thing to back up my claims.

"I only wanted you because you are my daughter. I wanted you Avidya, so I could finally get a foot in to places I couldn't before."

"You are one sick bastard," Taylor seethed. I couldn't agree more on that front. Was Taylor the only man that was sane in this family?

"Well, so are you, dear brother. So are you," Aaron said with a glare. "You wanted that slut of a girl that I had, so much so you tried to have me killed." Then turning back to me, "I would have given you such pleasure, you'd never want to leave, Avidya. You see, I wanted you for myself. And when Cody didn't show up with you in toe, I threatened him how I saw fit.

"He had as yet to get you to me, and now I'm not waiting any longer. So, to answer your question, Avidya. You are mine. I will take ya from this house, let you keep that *thing*, and you can play house all the while, and I'll have everything I ever want."

I shook my head. He was sick and twisted. He would never get me to leave this house unless I was dead.

Before I could react, Taylor sprang from the chair, knife in hand. He charged at Aaron, stabbing the knife deep into his gut.

"Fuck!" Aaron shouted as a gun went off.

Bang.

Both of my hands covered my mouth as I watched on in horror. Taylor's surprised face paled as blood instantly seeped from his chest. His legs gave out and he fell to the floor.

Aaron simply looked at him in disgust from where he stood, his own wound bleeding.

Oh God. Oh God. *Oh my God.*

Within seconds, the front door was busted down. Three men stormed into the house as though they owned it. They each had guns drawn.

I sat in horror. I didn't move. I *couldn't* as fear ran

down my spine.

"Ah, about time you came inside," Aaron said, his face beginning to pale from the pain and blood loss. "I knew that girl called. Someone had to. I saw you three out there, talking. I knew you would come in. Just a bit too late."

As he went to raise his gun, I knew he was going to shoot me next. I saw the dark look in his eyes. If he couldn't have me, no one would.

Before he was able to pull the trigger, all three men fired at Aaron, shooting him in the chest.

He fell in slow motion to the floor. His blood seeping into the carpet right along with Taylor's. One man kept his gun pointed at Aaron as he gasped for air on the floor as the other two men cleared the house. No one else was here, but I couldn't get my brain or mouth to work as I sat frozen in shock.

## Chapter 16

## Avidya

"Avidya?" asked a voice. A voice that I knew and hadn't heard for many months. Although he repeated my name at least three times, I couldn't get my eyes to move away from the two dead bodies.

Oh God.

Taylor was dead.

He was dead.

He couldn't be.

No.

Please. No.

"Avidya, honey," the voice spoke again. He moved, blocking my view of the bodies. I'd never get the view of them, the view of the blood, from my memory. How much more did I have to witness in my life?

I blinked my eyes, making his face come into focus.

Before me kneeled my brother. His eyes, dark with lack of sleep and worry, met mine. He looked at me as though he was afraid I'd fall apart.

I felt like I could.

My body was rocking slightly back and forth as

panic consumed me. Or was it shock? Shocked panic, maybe?

"There you are," he smiled sadly. "Are you okay?"

Was I okay?

I had no idea. How could I be after everything I've been through?

A sharp pain along my stomach caused me to groan out, folding over as the shooting pain took my breath away.

"Avidya?" Travis's voice reached me. He was worried, and rightfully so.

"I'm okay," I mumbled out as the pain passed.

"No, you aren't," Travis said as he stood. "I think you need to get checked out."

I shook my head as I sat fully back up. I was okay.

"We are at least going to go outside. I'll give you thirty minutes to prove me wrong, then," Travis stated, holding his hand out for me.

Slowly, I let him help me up. I was numb to everything; it was the only way I knew how to deal right now. After everything that had happened, I just didn't want to deal anymore.

Travis led me outside and helped me sit on the porch. He took a seat next to me, not saying anything. Was there anything that could be said?

I didn't think there was.

"Avidya?" Krissy came running across the yard to me. Her voice frantic. "Are you okay? What happened?"

"Pretty sure she's in shock," Travis answered for me.

"I heard gunshots. Are you okay? Where's Mr. Shantez?" Krissy fired off.

"He's . . . ." I was unable to finish as my tears fell.

"Oh, honey," Krissy said, instantly wrapping her arms around me. At the simple comforting touch, I burst into sobs. The kind that wracked my body with each passing second.

"I'll leave you two for a moment. Don't go anywhere," Travis said, standing up and making his way back into the house.

I don't know how long I cried against Krissy, but by the time I was able to get my emotions under control, a dull ache made itself known in my stomach once more. Pulling back, I wiped my eyes with the back of my hand.

"Sorry," I muttered.

"Don't you worry about that," Krissy said. "You okay? You're not hurt, are you?"

"I'm okay, I think," I sniffed.

"How far along is she?" Travis asked, appearing

back as quickly as he had left.

"Just about seven months," Krissy answered for me with a frown. "You would be?"

"Travis," he answered.

"Not the baby's father?" she asked.

"No," I answered right before another pang of pain grabbed ahold of me.

"I think she needs to be seen by the doctor," Travis said, watching as I fought against the pain.

"I agree," Krissy said. "But what about the police? Shouldn't they be here by now?"

"Eh, don't worry about that," Travis said, running a hand over his hair. "I got that covered. My buddies in there called it in."

"This is one of those things you don't want to know about," I gritted out as the pain lessoned.

She knew that there were a few things in my life that I couldn't talk about.

"Gotcha," Krissy said. "I'll take her to the ER to be checked over."

"She aint going anywhere without me," Travis said, easily taking the demanding role he was known well for.

"Don't tell Zach," I said, begging him.

"As long as you go get checked out," Travis said,

giving me a look that said to not push him.

"Okay. Thank you," I sighed. I'd do as they wanted, even though I was sure it would be for nothing.

For now, I'd let them have their way so I could forget about what sort of mess lay inside my home.

## Chapter 17

## Avidya

Maybe Travis and Krissy were right—I needed to be checked out. By the time we made it to the ER, my stomach was cramping too much, and too bad, to be able to just push it off as anything typical.

It hadn't taken long to get into the maternity ward, Krissy was at my side as Travis was forced to wait in the waiting room. The small room only fit one other person, as it was only meant to be used as a check in room. There was a small half bed, one chair, and a desk with a computer with monitors. The monitors had a number of wires that I wasn't too concerned about figuring out what was used for.

I answered all the needed questions about how far along I was, who my doctor was, and how long I had felt the contractions. The nurse didn't waste time to check and what I was feeling was in fact contractions, if the bands around my stomach said anything otherwise. I was too far dilated to try to stop the contractions.

I was in labor.

This was not how I was planning my day to go. None of it was. Would I be in labor if Aaron hadn't barged his way into my home? Would I have come in sooner if I had known about the possibility of going into labor so early?

"Let's get you into a room and I'll call your doctor. Give me five minutes. If you need me, just press that button right there and someone will be in soon," the nurse said.

Everything seemed to be such a blur. Maybe I was in shock. Maybe I had been dealt too much. Or maybe I was just tired of my life being so crappy constantly. There always seemed to be something right around the corner when I always thought that everything was going just perfect, or as close to perfect as possible.

"You'll be okay," Krissy said quietly next to me. "I won't leave. Unless you want me to."

"Stay, please," I asked, trying to hold all my emotions in. It was easier said than done.

"Of course," she said. "My parents have Catrina, so I can stay as long as needed."

"Thank you," I said, letting my body slightly relax. Although it didn't last as another strong contraction hit. It felt like my insides were being twisted together, and not in a good way.

As the contraction calmed, the nurse whisked back in with a wheelchair letting me know that they had a room all ready for me.

"Travis," I said, looking at Krissy. I needed my brother. If I couldn't have Zach, he'd do just fine.

"I'll get him," Krissy promised. "Let's get you to your room first."

I nodded as I moved from the bed to the wheelchair. There was no way I'd be able to walk with the pain, let alone with having a gown that showed off my backside to the world. The pressure down below was starting to draw my attention quickly, also.

Before I knew it, I was in a room, sitting on the bed, being re-hooked up to monitors of all kinds. Krissy stood next to me, holding my hand as the IV was inserted into my other hand. Travis stood off to the side, seeming shocked himself. His widened eyes were open, trying to take everything in.

"All set," the nurse smiled. "You're in good hands here, Avidya."

One white blanket laid across my legs as the nurse turned the volume up on the computer. The heartbeat of the baby filled the room, soothing me at least a little bit.

We were both okay.

"Are you sure you want me here?" Travis asked, looking around with a fearful look.

I could understand. I was scared myself. I never expected to be here so soon. I had no idea what to expect. I didn't know if we would both be okay.

"You don't have to be," I answered. "Just stay for a little bit. Please."

"Okay," Travis said, straightening his back. I could tell he was preparing himself for what was to come.

"So, what are you to Avidya?" Krissy asked.

"Her brother," Travis answered. "And I come to bring her back home, but I guess that'll have to wait."

"You are not taking her back there," Krissy said, placing her hands on her hips.

"I can't, Travis," I sighed out. "You know why, so don't even ask."

*Shit!* I cussed in my thoughts as another contraction hit. At the same moment, I felt like I peed myself. Double shit. Everything felt warm, grossly so.

"Uh…" I panted.

"You're okay. Your water broke," Krissy said, trying to hide her laugh as my disgusted look. "Totally normal."

"No worries. Let's get that cleaned up, and I'll see how far dilated you are," the nurse said softly.

Within minutes, and between contractions that

seemed to come on every two to ten minutes, the bedding was changed and I had a new blanket over my lap. And just in time for my doctor to come strolling through the door. She didn't take a second look at my brother or Krissy as she made her way to me.

"Hello, Avidya," she greeted. "Let's see how things are going."

"Okay," I muttered. Could it just all be over with already?

"You're about eight weeks early," she mused. "But nothing to worry about. The baby will need some extra time in the NICU, but normal for this early. A station is being set up now as I speak. Just be prepared that the baby will most likely be whisked away out of the room before you can hold him. Nothing to worry about, and everyone here will keep you updated on him every step of the way."

"Will she be okay?" Travis asked, hands stuffed into his pockets.

"I don't see any reason she won't be," Dr. Fare answered as she slipped gloves over her hands to check.

Thankfully, she waited for the contraction to pass before checking me.

"I'll give you about another hour or so before this little one is born. Pretty fast for the first baby," she laughed.

"Oh, God. I was in labor for over three days," Krissy groaned out. "Wish mine was this fast."

"I'm assuming you've been in labor most of the day, actually. You seem to handle pain well," the doctor stated.

At the words, I couldn't stop the blush from spreading. She had no idea how much pain my husband once said he wanted to inflict me. Not bad pain, but pleasuring pain.

As another contraction hit, Travis and my doctor introduced themselves to one another. I didn't pay attention to what either of them said as I concentrated on the pain, willing it to go away. It was too late to have any sort of pain reliever.

*Oh God!*

I felt like I was going to die.

## Chapter 18
## Avidya

Four hours later, which felt like a lifetime after everything that had happened, I sat in the NICU, watching my little baby boy in the hospital bed. The glass surrounded the baby, but allowed for someone to be able to reach in through the side to touch the baby. The nurses called the baby beds a giraffe bed, although I wasn't sure why they used name, at least it worked,

My baby was wrapped lightly, cords were just about everywhere. It would have been scary if I hadn't known what I was walking into. It *was* scary, but thankfully the nurse had explained to me what I was about to see before I was allowed in. Still, nothing would have been able to prepare me to see my helpless child in such a way.

I could hardly stop the tears of relief and sadness for everything that had happened in such a short time.

The labor pains were so horribly bad, no book, no other mother, could ever tell you just how bad it was. It was nearly burning from the inside out with no relief to be found. At all. Not even squeezing the life out of Krissy and Travis' hands helped.

Now, I was just so freaking tired, but I couldn't

sleep. Not until I was able to see my baby. Joshua Taylor. He looked so small, though, now that I got to see him.

He had been whisked off right after the umbilical cord had been cut. As I had begun to push him out, his heart rate kept dropping. It had been too late to do a C-section at that time, but I was so tired, I had to have help to finish getting him out. The doctor had taken to using a clamp to pull him out as my contractions continued on.

No one ever told me it would be so hard.

Looking through the glass that kept my baby safe and warm, the heart monitor tracking the heartbeat, I was finally able to relax slightly. Not as well as I could if I was able to hold him, but at least it was better than nothing. He was alive, and that was more than I could ever ask for.

I had been so close to losing my life just hours ago, and now here I was staring at the life I gave.

His eyes were closed as he slept. He had a feeding tube in and oxygen tubes in his nose. My heart hurt for him, but I knew he didn't feel any pain. He was just a little over three pounds, and had a few weeks to go before he'd be released.

"You must be his mother," spoke a nurse as she came up to check on my baby.

"Yeah," I whispered tiredly.

"He's doing well so far," she said. "I'm Hope. And I'll be watching over him tonight. First time mother?" she guessed after she fiddled with a few of the machines and wires.

"That obvious?" I laughed, looking at her for a moment.

She was easily ten years older than me with her black hair pulled back into a low ponytail. Her green eyes were filled with compassion.

"He's in good hands here," she said, giving my shoulder a pat. "Eight weeks early is nothing to worry about. I've been there, and although I know it doesn't work, try to rest. That way you can be ready for those sleepless nights that will be coming when he's released."

"If only I could sleep," I yawned out.

"Your doctor can help. It'd be good. You look like you've walked through Hell," she said, trying to brighten my mood.

"Oh, I have," I said sadly. "I lost my uncle today, too."

"Oh, honey. I'm so sorry," she said. She sounded like it too.

I could only shrug, feeling tears prickle my eyes once more. Hadn't I cried enough already?

"Things have to start looking up sometime. Do you have family here?" she asked.

"Yeah," I sniffed. "My brother. He went to get me some clothes and lock up the house."

The same house I wasn't sure I'd ever be able to step into again. But I wanted my own clothes to walk the halls in instead of this flimsy hospital gown.

How much of a mess was the house in? Did I even want to know?

No. No I didn't.

"He's not going to go anywhere," she stated. "Go rest, honey. If anything changes, I'll give your room number a call."

"How long will he be in here?" I asked. I had to know.

"All depends on him. He has to be able to eat on his own and maintain his body temperature. Could be a couple of days up to a few weeks. It all depends on the baby. And each baby is different," she answered.

"Okay, thank you," I whispered.

Pushing myself up from the chair, I gave Joshua one last look before trekking back to my room. Somehow, the nurse was able to put me to ease enough that maybe I'd be able to get a bit of sleep. Still think it was likely to get much after everything had happened within less than twelve hours.

How did other parents do all this? Did they lose a family member and gain one at the same time? How was I going to handle all this? I never let the thought of having a preemie. Everything had gone so well the entire pregnancy, so I never expected things to turn out this way. Maybe fate had stepped in for a reason now instead of waiting for another few weeks.

Was it because of the shock I had been through? Was my body just not able to handle anything else?

I had no idea.

What I did know is that I wished that I had my family here to keep me company and tell me that everything would be fine. I wanted Zachariah. I wanted to go home. I just wanted things to be different than what they were.

None of those options were likely once more.

Once I was back in my room, taking a slow walk the entire way because my body wouldn't let me go much faster, I found it to be empty, just as I had left it. Travis wasn't back yet, and wouldn't be until morning since it was past visiting hours. Krissy went home to sleep since it wasn't often she had a kid-free night.

I had promised them all I would be perfectly fine on my own, but now I wished one of them had been determined to stay with me. I just really didn't want to be alone, despite what I had said earlier.

Surprisingly, it didn't take me long to doze off on the uncomfortable bed with a blanket pulled up to my chin. I'd been walking around with the blanket over my shoulders to hide the gown that I wanted to change out of.

Soon. Soon I'd get better clothes and shower.

For now, I'd live with what I did have. I had a baby. I still had family. And I was still alive.

What more could I ask for?

## Chapter 19

## Zachariah

The sun was just peeking over the horizon when my cell phone rang. I glared at it. Not because it woke me, but because I wanted to be left alone. If my glare could burn it into ashes, it would already be smoke blowing in the wind.

It had been three days since Travis had called, and he was no closer to getting my wife back home and in one piece. He wouldn't even tell me what town he was in so I could come do it myself. He only gave me the brief words that 'now isn't the time.' What was that supposed to mean? It was past time! I wasn't paying him to just go on vacation.

"What?" I barked out.

"Figured you'd be up," Carlos answered in way of greeting. "I will be going out of town for a few days. Some of my men came across a snitch and I need to make sure the clean-up crew do their job."

"And why are you telling me this?" I asked, confused.

"Because I know you are following my tracks, that's why," my dad answered with heat, not pleased I was doing so. "Plus, your mother will be going along with me. Something about wanting a vacation."

"Fine," I breathed. What did I care? Why won't everyone just leave me, then?

"I expect you to behave and keep things under control," Dad went on. "I should be back by this time next week or so."

"Got it," I spoke. "Anything else?"

"That's all," he said.

I didn't give him a chance to say anything else as I hung up the phone.

My father was getting on my last nerve. He wanted me to do everything for him, it seemed. I understood that he was just trying to keep my mind busy so I didn't do something stupid. I did want to do something stupid, many things. But he made sure I had no time to do anything of that sort.

Did he purposely tell me he was leaving town because he knew I'd follow his moves, or because he wanted to see what I'd do? I would have followed him if he hadn't have told me, because I would take any lead right now that I possibly could.

There wasn't much I could do if he was leaving me in charge of everything. I had to stay here and be the good son he expected me to be. Besides, I already had Travis on the job.

Sighing, I ran my hand down my face. I wondered if anything would have been different if I never met Avidya. What would I be doing if she had never fallen into my lap as she did? Would I have ever come across a woman to marry? Probably not. I couldn't see myself marrying anyone other than Avidya. She was it for me.

I wasn't going to let her go that easily, either. I just had to come up with the perfect way to get her back, other than dragging her ass back home. I would if I had to, but I wanted to try to get her to see I couldn't live without her.

In the kitchen, I made a cup of coffee. I had a number of interviews for the club today for new members. It was not something I was looking forward to, that was for sure. So many people were too new to the lifestyle, and had warped views of how things were supposed to be in my place. They all had to learn the hard way. Either agree to follow my rules that I had lined out, or don't apply to become a member.

Pretty simple.

Only crappy thing was that most of the men I was doing business with under the brothel name wanted in. I couldn't willingly allow them in knowing what they were after. I didn't ever want to mix that with business. Some people didn't understand BDSM wasn't a game; it is a lifestyle I was starting to get the itch to start a brothel back up just to keep that high money coming in.

Almost.

As the coffee pot finished brewing my java, my phone once again rang.

Groaning, I answered, my words short and to the point. "What now?"

"Not a good morning, I take it?" Travis's voice came through.

"What do you want?" I repeated. I wasn't up to playing games right now. He sure as fuck knew that too.

"I just wanted to let you know that Avidya is sick and won't be able to come back right away. Nothing life threatening," he hurriedly explained. "I'm going to stick around for another day or so just to make sure. But she promised she'd think about returning when she feels up to traveling."

"Sick with what?" I barked. She wasn't the type to get sick at the drop of a pen. Was she really sick? Was she just not wanting me to see me again? Had I possibly ruined whatever we once had?

"Just this sickness that is going around. She works

at a daycare center, so she assumes she picked up one of the many bugs," Travis said.

I could picture him shrugging on the other end of the phone as he sat in his car.

"I'll let you know when she's up to seeing you, though," he went on. "When I came back, I'll give you her location and you can come see her. Talk to her."

"Alright," I sighed out. That, that I could handle. I'd go and beg her to fucking take me back. I couldn't live without her any more. "You sure she's okay?"

"Yeah," Travis answered. "Her friend got hurt, so she's worried about that. But she's okay."

"Okay. Keep me posted," I sighed.

"Will do," he said, ending the call.

Well, at least things couldn't get any worse, could they?

~oOo~

I had spoken too soon.

Things did get worse. Much worse.

An hour later, as I pulled up to the club, I couldn't help but let a round of cuss words fall from my mouth. I thought Avidya leaving me was bad, but this topped the list. I no longer knew what the fuck to do. My life was falling apart everywhere I looked.

Firetrucks. Police tape. Sirens. Lights. Smoke. Water.

My heart couldn't take anymore. I was done with everything.

My club was burnt to ashes.

Only thing left standing was the walls, but even they were covered in water and soot.

Smoke billowed up into the sky as if it was finished destroying the rest of my life that was worthwhile.

Someone set my place on fire. And they would pay for doing so.

Cooling my pure rage and fury, I stepped out of my parked car, drawing attention to the nearest firefighter and cop as they stood back, watching to make sure the place was as safe as it possibly could be in its current state.

"You the owner?" the cop asked, tipping his head up to meet my eyes.

"Yes. Zachariah Melendez," I answered. "What happened here?" I nodded my chin towards my building.

"We got the call about three hours ago for the fire, and by then the place wasn't salvageable. No one was in there, but from the looks of it, the fire started in the back room," the firefighter answered. "I believe this fire was started by an arsonist."

"Just fucking great," I mumbled to myself. I ran a hand down harshly over my face, willing life to just let something go right for once for me.

"Do you have anyone that would want to burn this place down, or someone who wanted to hurt you?" the cop asked.

"Everyone wants to hurt me and my family," I deadpanned.

He must have been new to the task force, as it was pretty common my family was either hated or looked up to.

"Alright," the cop said, fear starting to make its way through his body. "We'll check the cameras and see if there's any video showing who started the fire."

"Why didn't my fire alarm go off?" I asked. I had every safety measure in place, there shouldn't have been any way a fire could have been set unless someone knew the inner workings of my building.

"Not sure, sir," the cop replied. "Could it have been one of your employees?"

"No," I said with a shake of my head. "Only three employees know how to disarm it. One of which is not in town right now. The other I trust to keep this place opened

"If you think of anyone, give the station a call," the cop said, making his way to his car. Yeah, he was new.

Pulling my phone from my pocket, I called Jonas. I knew he wouldn't do this, but he may have an idea who did. I would hunt who burned my club to the ground and they would pay for doing so.

Luckily, Jonas picked up on the first ring. "Sir?"

"The club is closed. It's burnt down to the ground," I said, making my way to my car.

"What? No way!" Jonas said, sounding appalled and pissed at the same time.

"Yeah. Some fucker set it on fire," I said.

"Any idea who?" Jonas asked, still trying to process what I had just told him.

"That's why I called you," I stated, my voice hard. I was not in the mood to play around.

"I'll look into it," Jonas said. "No one was there when I left last night. Possibly could be one of the men that wants in but wasn't allowed a membership."

"Most likely," I huffed. "Just not sure which one. There's a few of them I won't ever allow in."

"Well, at least you have the casinos," Jonas said. "It's not like you're losing money. Insurance will kick in and you can rebuild or buy a new place."

"The casinos are all under the Don's care," I explained. "But yes. I will restart it up after the fucker is caught. You know what to do you when you find him."

"Got it, boss," Jonas said, hanging up with a click.

I could easily get into the casinos and help run them, but my father had that handled without me. We protected our own, and I wouldn't hesitate to step up if needed. But I wanted my own well known business outside of the Las Vegas strip. I wanted to have my own say on how I could do things.

And now it was burnt down to the ground.

It wouldn't be for long. Oh no.

First thing first, file a claim, then start looking for a place that would be bigger and better.

No one would bring me down this way. I would be coming back, stronger than ever.

## Chapter 20

## Avidya

Two days later, I was released from the hospital and in my own clothes. I didn't want to be released, exactly. I couldn't walk in that door and know that Taylor wouldn't be coming home after me. The house would be empty, cold of the man I had grown close to over the past six months.

It was a love hate relationship.

I wanted to sleep in my own bed. I wanted to take my baby home with me, too. But I couldn't.

Joshua was doing very well, despite everything. He was still in the NICU with oxygen and a feeding tube. I had high hopes that he'd be able to get off of all the machines in as little as a few weeks. He certainly put up a fight against every little thing already.

The only thing that I was looking forward to was that I wouldn't be interrupted every hour by a nurse. And I would be getting to hold Joshua today for the very first time. I couldn't wait for that, even with all the cords hooked up to my little baby.

Right after being released, and making sure I had everything I needed, I made my way to the NICU, that was luckily a part of the maternity ward. I was still sore and not able to walk as fast as I normally would have been able to, but I still walked from my room to the nursery at least three or four times a day.

What else did I have to do?

No one ever told me how tough the after-birth process was. It was almost nearly as bad as giving birth over and over. Okay, maybe not that bad, but the cramps were not fun, that was for sure. I couldn't take a bath to help ease the pains, and Advil only dulled it. Not nearly enough to help, though.

I was certain I was not going to have any more children for many years. Experiencing all this, alone, was more than enough for me for a lifetime.

"Hello, Miss," greeted one of the nurses.

I gave her a small smile as I sat down my overnight bag by the wall.

"Which one is yours?" she asked.

"She's Joshua's mom," stated the nurse I had first met here. She had been a lifesaver. Since I had first sat next to my son, she had told me she had been in my shoes, and that helped more than any other nurse here could ever say to me.

"Oh," replied the first nurse. "He is so cute. He's

doing very well today."

"You ready to hold him?" Nurse Hope asked.

"Yes," I answered with a bigger smile.

"Perfect. Go have a seat in the chair while I get him ready for you," she said.

I took a seat in the chair I normally sat in when I came to see my son. It was just like the rocking chair that went unused in my hospital room. The cushioned cover was green and blue, matching the colors of this part of the hospital.

Once I was sitting, the nurse was there, opening the compartment that my son was in, being careful of all the cords and wires he was hooked up to.

"You ready?" she asked.

"So much so," I breathed out.

I couldn't wait to hold the little one in my arms. I was ready. For a new start in life with my little baby. It was really all I had now.

Within minutes, Joshua was in my arms laying his head on my chest. He was so little against me. So small and warm. His little lungs took in air as he breathed in the scent of me.

My heart swelled being able to hold him finally. I would never put him down.

"I'll be back in a little while," the nurse smiled before making her way back to check on other little babies.

I so hoped that everything would go smoothly and I could take him home sooner rather than later. I was literally holding my reason for everything in my arms, and I silently promised him that I would do everything in my power to make sure he had a happy, safe, life.

~oOo~

"You ready?" Travis asked as he shut the car off in front of the house.

"As ready as I'll ever be," I sighed out, wishing the past week couldn't have happened. I glared at the house, willing it to change things from how it all happened.

"It's okay," he said, patting my knee. "Everything's been cleaned up. And Krissy was determined to set up a nursery, sorta. She's a determined girl."

"She usually is," I laughed. I don't know what I would have done without her by my side.

I was glad I had a friend here. She was possibly the only thing keeping me sane at the moment. She had come to visit me every day so far, although she wasn't allowed into the NICU because she wasn't the father. Travis was allowed in, since the nurse felt bad that the father wasn't there with me, and he was my brother. He wasn't able to hold Joshua, but he'd get the chance to soon enough.

"Come on," he said as he began to get out of the car.

I slowly followed him. My heart sped up, fearing that I'd relive the horrible thing over again. It was the shock of it all, mostly. I don't think I've fully processed that Taylor was no longer alive.

Travis was patient as I slowly made my way up to the house. I almost would have rather walked back into Zach's house.

Almost.

I wasn't quite ready to step over that small, but huge, hurdle quite yet.

Once I reached the step, the door was opened, a smiling Krissy on the other side. Before I could react, she had me wrapped in her arms, giving me a hug that I didn't know I needed.

"Please don't be mad," she whispered in my ear. "Travis made a few phone calls."

"I can't promise that," I muttered as she pulled back, but then she took ahold of my hand. "What did you do?"

She gave me a small, encouraging smile before dragging me into the house. Once inside, Krissy came to stop, and my breath left my lungs. I could have collapsed in shock and joy if Travis hadn't been behind me.

Inside the house, there stood Carlos and Julia. I probably should have expected Carlos to show up because of what happened, but I never expected Julia of all people.

"Julia," I cried, rushing to pull her into a hug. I was so happy to see her after so long. Talking to her on the phone was good, but seeing her in person was so much better.

"Hello, dear," she said, returning my hug.

We held onto one another for a few more moments before I pulled back, wiping away my tears. Damn my stupid hormones.

"How are you?" she asked, looking me up and down.

"Better now that you're here," I answered truthfully.

"You look tired," she stated.

"I am, but I don't think I can sleep," I said.

"Sit, sit," she said, taking a seat on the couch, that I noticed was brand new. And so was the carpet and painted walls. Looking around, no one would be able to tell that two people were shot and killed in this house. Everything was clean and almost brand new.

At that thought, a shiver ran through me.

"So tell me, when does my grandson get to come home?" Julia asked.

"A few weeks," I shrugged. "Hopefully. He's doing well, considering he was born so early."

"I don't doubt that he'll be just fine," she said. "I'll be here for a while to help, if you'll let me."

"Really?" I asked, surprised. Would she really be able to stay and keep Zach from finding out?

"Yes," she smiled. "Carlos wouldn't have offered to bring me along if he thought otherwise. You've been through so much. It's the least I could do to help. And I'm sure you won't want Zach here, or for him to find out, yet. Do you?"

"Not yet," I said, shaking my head. I did want him to show up, but with so much going on lately, I just wanted a few more weeks to myself. "If he finds me on his own, then I can handle it. But I'm not ready for more stress just yet."

"Then that's what we'll do," Julia said. "Let me help you. We are all here for you. I know that being a new mother is hard, even with help. So, please, let me stay a week or two."

"I will only be able to be here for another day or so before I have to get back," Carlos stated. "But there shouldn't be any more threats against you. Ever."

"Good," I said, my voice hard.

Maybe things could start being better now that Aaron was no longer alive. Maybe life would be on the right path now as things calmed down and I got to figure out how to live a life of less threats.

I knew that Taylor didn't want a funeral, or anything for that matter. There would be no goodbye for him. I knew that life would keep on going, no matter what had happened in this house. But, everything would be fine in the end.

I could do this mother thing. I had family that was willing to help, and a few good friends. So things would work out, one way or another.

## Chapter 21

### Avidya

Five weeks.

Five weeks seemed so pass extremely slow.

Five weeks my baby was in the NICU.

Five weeks to the day, I was finally able to bring him home.

Five weeks.

I never knew how horrible five weeks would have been, or how wonderful it was at the same time. So much had changed in such a short amount of time. So much so, I didn't know how I lived as I had before becoming a mother.

All my thoughts had been on my son, worrying about things that probably didn't even need to be worried about.

Julia was a constant presence in the house, helping me clean and buy clothes for the baby. He had more than enough clothes to last for many years, all ranging from different sizes.

In the bedroom I had taken over, there had been a few changes to fit the small portable crib that Taylor had bought me not all that long ago. It fit into the room perfectly, and would work until Joshua was about six months or so.

He had taken to feeding from a bottle like a pro, and was off the oxygen without any issues. Surprisingly, he was doing very well still being so early. It was still a week away from my official due date, but Joshua was cleared and ready to go home.

I had spent every day at his side, helping the nurses to care for him. The only reason I ever went home was to sleep and get some needed *me* time before I had no more time to do that.

I was ready for my son to be home. I was ready to introduce him to the world. I was ready to be a full-time mother that came along with having my child at home with me.

Yes, Julia would still be around for another week, mostly because she wanted to hold and spoil the little man. That I couldn't agree more on.

I knew that when Travis and Julia would return back home, it would only be a matter of time before Zachariah showed up. And I was okay with that.

I was ready for him to come find me. I was ready for him to know why I hid this secret from him for so long.

I was ready to be a family of three.

I was ready to face him once and for all.

It didn't take that long to get the car seat secured into the car that Travis was currently using, and the same car that would be left for me to use after he went back home. Julia had gone with us, having Travis drive us all to the hospital to get my baby and then back home.

Krissy had wanted to be home, but she had to work. She promised that she'd stop by later, though. Catrina also couldn't wait to meet the baby, as she wasn't allowed to be inside the hospital due to all the sickness going around.

Having Julia with me the past few weeks was nice, though. Having someone to talk to and knowing I wasn't left alone was a blessing. She even went to church with me every Sunday.

"How long do you think it'll take Zach to find me?" I asked after we got back home and settled in.

"I'll give him maybe two weeks tops to get here," Travis joked. "At the moment, he's a bit busy. But once he gets the issue taken care of, he will be here as fast as possible."

"And you won't tell him the exact location," Julia said, giving him a look that said not to try.

"Just the town," Travis said with an eyeroll. "And

nothing about the package."

Travis had mentioned that my husband was busy with something, but didn't tell me what. At least Zach seemed to be in a better mood after so many months. Maybe he finally started to act his age and get things done.

"He has taken time to cool down, so I'm sure he won't do something stupid," Travis said, not taking his eyes of my son sleeping in my arms.

I had no idea what to expect when he showed up, but I was ready. I was ready to hear his side, and hopefully explain my side as well as I could. I did expect him to be mad at me and not let me explain. I could understand his anger that would no doubt come along with his reappearance.

That I could handle.

I just didn't think I could handle him wanting nothing to do with me anymore because I had a kid. Would he demand I give him up? Because I would never do such a thing.

He'd have to accept us both, or neither of us. He couldn't just have one without the other. I didn't care if it broke my heart again, but my son was my life. I ran to have him, and I would stop at nothing to make sure it stayed that way.

Julia was on my side, and the more people I had, the better.

"Did you get everything you'll need?" Travis asked, helping himself to the very well-stocked fridge.

"I think so," I answered as Julia took my son out of his seat.

In the corner by the couch was a baby swing, waiting to be used, along with a few other little baby things that had been scattered across the house.

It finally felt lived in.

I think there was almost too much stuff, now.

After being in this house for over six months, the place finally felt like home. Or, well, as close as much as it could. I needed Zachariah here with me to make it complete, because he was home to me, but I could handle all this that was here.

"You okay?" Julia asked, cocking her head to the side in worry.

"Yeah, sorry," I said, clearing my head. "Just thinking."

"I'm here if you want to talk," Julia said as she took a seat on the couch after taking Joshua from my arms.

"I'm alright," I sighed. "Just thinking about things that are out of my control."

"Alright," Julia said, letting it go for now.

"How's Toby doing?" I missed him, too. How was he handling me gone for so long? I was, after all, the only person that he had gotten along with at the first moment he met them. I took a seat on the couch.

"He's doing okay," Julia said. "He's dealing, I guess. Going to therapy, but still not happy about you leaving. He thinks that it was all Zach's fault that you left."

"But it wasn't," I said. "When you go back, please let him know that I will be home soon. And that I miss him?"

"Of course," Julia said. "He'd be very happy to hear that. But he'd be happier if you called him and told him yourself."

I made a mental note to talk to him when I went back home. I just hoped he could forgive me, too. He may be harder to gain back on my side than my own husband.

It wasn't that long after that Krissy showed up, Catrina in tow. The little girl bounced with each step she took, happy to see me and Joshua.

Once her eyes landed on the baby, they widened and she froze for a second before a splitting grin met her lips.

"Can I hold him?" she asked.

"Not yet," Krissy said. "He's really small. When he gets a bit older, then you can. Okay?"

"Oh. Okay," she sighed sadly.

"But you can touch his hand or foot. That'd be okay, Catrina," I smiled.

"Can you have a baby, Mommy?" Catrina asked her mother.

"One is perfect for me," Krissy laughed. Then, turning to me she asked "How are you doing?"

"Happy to not have to be at the hospital every day," I said through a yawn.

"I bet so," she laughed, taking a seat on the floor and making herself at home. She stole one of the chips off my plate that sat on the table next to me in the process.

"Do you always just help yourself to whatever?" Travis asked jokingly as he eyed my friend.

"What's wrong with that?" she asked. "You stole her food."

"So. I'm her brother," Travis shot back.

"How's Kenna?" I asked, trying to change the subject.

"Wonderful," Travis said, wagging his eyebrows.

"How can you stand letting a woman boss you around?" Krissy asked.

She knew the lifestyle that I had, and vaguely understood Travis' sex life. That had been a slightly awkward conversation about stuff I didn't really know about.

I just knew that I liked submitting to my husband in the bedroom only. I was not the type to let him control everything I did, and he knew that too.

"It's easy," Travis shrugged. "It's not a full day and night thing. Well, not always. If we feel the need and just need to feel better after a rough day, or week, then we sit down and talk about it. We have completely free communication without jumping to conclusions."

"Still, it's all strange," Krissy hummed.

"At first, yes," I answered. "But it does grow on you. It did on me."

"Of course, the BDSM lifestyle isn't for everyone," Travis said. "It all depends on the person."

"What about you, Julia?" Krissy asked.

"I prefer to not partake in this conversation," Julia answered, although she had a slight smile on her face.

"She's not very kinky," Travis muttered on a laugh.

"No, that I am not," Julia agreed. "But that doesn't mean I haven't dabbled."

"Ew!" Travis said, covering his ears.

All us girls burst out laughing.

## Chapter 22

### Zachariah

I was at a loss for words. There was nothing I could possibly do as I stood, trying to blend in with all the other people that were out and about on this nice warm spring day. I couldn't believe that she was here, almost within reach.

She sat on the bench, next to a woman that had red hair who had a little red haired girl chatting away instead of playing with the other kids who were playing on the slides and jungle gym. A black stroller sat in front of both women.

From where I stood, I wasn't able to hear them. I wished that I could. I should just step up and show myself. Instead, I stayed put, watching the love of my life.

She looked perfectly healthy and untouched. Her light blond hair was pulled back into a high ponytail, showing off her slender neck. She looked happy. How could she after we had been apart for so long? She couldn't have forgotten me, could she?

My heart, which had yet to heal, broke again. How could she be so happy? Didn't she suffer from leaving me?

How could she willingly give up on us, run away, and look like nothing had happened between us?

I couldn't believe it had been almost seven months ago that she left me without a word. Her wedding ring was burning a hole in my pocket, as I refused to go anywhere without it.

She said something to the little girl, and finally, she ran off to play with a couple of other children.

I slowly made my way to her, being mindful I couldn't be seen. Not yet. I had to make sure I would be welcomed. It had been so long. It felt like years to me when it had only been a little less than a year since I saw her.

What was I planning to do? I had no idea. I didn't know what the right thing to do was. Would she even hear me out? Would Avidya want to see me? Or would she kick me in the balls and demand a divorce?

I had promised myself that I would just see her. I didn't plan to ever approach her. Not until I knew what I was walking into. I had no idea if she moved on with another man. I had no idea if that would even be a question. We were still fucking married, for God's sake!

There was a tree behind the bench Avidya sat on. I took the chance to sit down, leaning against it so I could hear what they were saying. I kept my face hidden under my hat. The green grass was slightly damp from this morning's watering, but it was the least of my concerns.

Luckily, I wore shorts and a loose shirt, so I looked just like a jogger. No one would know it was me.

No one even knew I was here. Not my father. Not my brother. Not even my guards. I was here as secretly as my wife was. Except for Travis, he knew since he had told me the town my wife had been in from the start.

The past couple of years had been some of the roughest years I'd ever gone through. I never thought I'd be able to find love. I never thought I'd find the reason to live.

I did. And it was everything more than I ever thought it could possibly be.

But with love came defeat and loneliness.

My world came crashing down in a matter of minutes when the love of my life left me, leaving a simple note and the wedding ring right there on my pillow for me to find. And without any reason from her. She never gave me any clue. Nothing.

It was by chance that I found out where my wife had been hiding. Travis had come back almost three weeks ago with the town and state that Avidya was staying in. He didn't give me any information on her health or reasons why he had stayed. He only told me that I'd see and understand myself when I went to get her. He also told me that I better return with her if I wanted to live.

I think he threatened to kill me, but I let it pass.

This time.

He wouldn't be so lucky the next time he made such a threat as that. I think he was in the doghouse with his Mistress as it was.

"So glad you are doing so well," the redhead said, seemingly happy about the fact.

"Me too. I'm so glad that everything is finally looking up," Avidya's voice said. It was still as soft and sweet as I remember.

"I still can't believe that you went through all of that and are still be able to stand," redhead spoke. "Do you plan to start working again?"

What had my wife been through?

"I've thought about it," Avidya answered. "I don't know yet, for sure. It's not like I need the money, but I can't be in that house. It's hard enough to just sleep there most nights since everyone has left. Not that I get sleep as it is." She laughed at the end, like it was expected to not be getting any sleep.

"You know you are more than welcome to stay with me and Catrina," red-head said. "I'm here if you want to talk. Heck, I'll even watch Josh for you. I know how hard it is, Vidie. I'm still there and will be for who knows how long."

"You could have just about any man, Krissy," Avidya laughed. "I bet any man out here jogging would love to have you. And your kid too." She looked around, easily spotting a number of men that were running on the sidewalk not that far away.

"I could say to same to you," the redhead replied with a laugh.

I could picture my wife blushing at the comment, and a small smile graced my lips.

"You know I can't," Avidya said with a small shake of her head.

"Any idea when he'll show up? Has Travis said anything?" Krissy asked.

"No," Avidya said, her voice low with defeat. "I should have just called him, but I just couldn't bring myself to do it. He'll hate me. Hell, I could only get myself talked into calling him that one time."

I didn't hate her. I was angry, yes. But I didn't hate her. I had so many questions about why she was here of all places. I wanted to know why she seemed to have gone through such a tragic event that no one told me about.

What had I missed the past half year?

"You can't hide from him forever," Krissy said. "You should let him know. He deserves it."

"If only it was that easy," Avidya sighed. It sounded as though she feared my reaction. She had nothing to fear from me.

The past few months, I had changed. Not sure if it was for the better or worse, but I had changed. I was so depressed. I did so many shitty things, one after another. I had been at my lowest point in life. All because of a woman.

Yet she sat there, and didn't seem to have to dealt with any of the things I did. She kept on living like nothing had happened.

"Someone came to kill me, Krissy. The only family member by blood that still cared for me was killed because he tried to protect me," Avidya said. She talked as though this was nothing out of the ordinary for her. "My life is so messed up, no one deserves me."

"But you fought every step of the way," Krissy said. "You deserve the entire world. Don't doubt yourself. Everyone that has met you loves you. Can't you see that? Taylor may have died to protect you, but you are so strong. He may have died to keep you alive, but you learned so much from him. You are that strong woman you should have been all these years.

"Do what your heart wants, not your mind. As long as you keep in touch with me, of course," she ended.

"I've let so many people down already, Krissy," Avidya said sadly. I heard the tears in her voice and I was just barely able to keep myself in place. I wanted to wrap my arms around her, taking all the hurt away.

"But they understood," Krissy said. "Didn't they?"

"Kinda," Avidya shrugged out. "The family that does know understands. You saw how Julia and Travis were last week."

"Seriously!" Krissy shouted, causing the baby in the stroller to let out a whimper. "Sorry."

I turned my head, watching as Avidya was quick to pick up the baby, who was no older than maybe two months, out of the stroller, shushing the thing.

*What the hell?*

My eyes widened in surprise as Avidya picked up the baby as though she knew exactly how to handle it. I wasn't surprised by that. What surprised me was the pale green eyes that locked with my own as the baby looked over Avidya's shoulder, looking at me as though it knew the exact reason why my wife left me.

It couldn't be.

No.

My chest felt tight as realization dawned on me.

"How could you not tell them? Any of them?" the redhead went on

"He wouldn't understand," Avidya answered. "I can't...I couldn't let him know. He would have taken Joshua from me. Or worse"

"How would you know?" Krissy asked, appalled.

"You haven't met him," Avidya said. "You haven't met my husband that wanted nothing to do with children. He told me once that he would do anything to make sure that I was not able to have a child, and I believed him."

"But you love them all!" Krissy hissed out.

"Very much. Each and every one of them," Avidya said. "I can't see any good it would do. It'd just break me more."

She didn't look broken, so what the fuck was she talking about?

"Then why hide the fact you had a kid? Why not let them know? They certainly care about you. I have seen those two men that come by at least every other week since you arrived to this town. They care for you," Krissy said.

"They are the only ones that know, and won't tell

anyone else," Avidya said fondly. "If it wasn't for the one getting me here, I wouldn't even have this little one."

"But you said he wasn't abusive," Krissy stated. "He'd certainly change his mind now."

"My...he doesn't like kids," Avidya stated, her voice turning cold.

"But you love him. I can see how much you miss him," Krissy said, clearly not getting the point. Neither was I. "Why can't you just give him a chance?"

"I do love him," she sighed out. "But this is my choice. If he wants to find me, he can. I won't fight. I won't throw a fit. I'll let him do whatever he wants. But he hasn't come to find me, Krissy. There's been no sign of him anywhere for the entire time I've been here." She paused, moving the baby down from her shoulder and laying him back into the stroller.

My mind still hadn't processed that I was a father. I was the father, wasn't I? I was sure no one could be, but still . . . .

How the fuck had no one told me?

"Why hasn't he shown up, do you think?" Krissy mused.

"I'm guessing no one has told him," Avidya shrugged. "Or maybe he has more important things to take care of. I'm surprised, actually. I've been expecting him to come at any moment since that first day I got here to drag me back home. But day after day, he hasn't shown up.

"I can't help but wonder if maybe he let me go without a fight," she finished quietly.

If only she knew the half of it. I would have come sooner if I had known.

"Are you better off being here on your own, then?" Krissy asked.

"I have no idea," Avidya said. "I miss being home. I miss having a family. But I gave that all up to have this little one. I have no idea what would even be left if I went back now."

Not able to take any more, I pushed myself up and stood. Taking one last look at what I knew I would never be able to erase from my mind, I began to walk away. I had a child. Avidya made her choice, and I'd honor it.

For now.

## Chapter 23

## Avidya

Going home to an empty house didn't sound all that appealing. After spending some time out with Krissy and Catrina—lunch and then to the park—I knew I had to go home. I needed to get some laundry washed, and also needed a nap. Possibly not in that order, either.

Joshua was not a night sleeper. The saying of sleep when the baby sleeps was not easy to follow. I tried, but it seemed even during the day he wanted to be held to sleep. Not that I minded, but I feared that I would hurt him if I fell asleep while holding him.

The baby swing was a godsend! Well, so were Krissy and Julia, before she left. I would be able to get a slight doze that would be considered a small nap during the day to help keep me going.

I had sent Julia home last week, needing some time to come to terms with what my life would consist of next. I knew things would be changing once more, because they always did.

It was only a matter of time.

Krissy now knew my entire life story, or pretty

close to it. I left out that Zach had gotten me as a *gift* that he kept. She didn't need to know that part. The rest she found out. Julia ended up telling her most of it, and I added in what she wasn't able to here and there.

Julia explained that the family was in a business, but left out the whole mafia part of it. That was for the best anyhow. I'd have hated putting Krissy and her daughter at risk because someone came looking for information.

My new friend took it all with an open mind. She didn't look at me differently. She simply gave me a hug and told me things would get better.

The past didn't define me, nor would it ever.

With Krissy knowing what I was hiding from, or more like who to an extent, I didn't have to hold back anymore on what I said to her. I never did in the first place, really. I just could answer some of her questions more easily.

Before having Joshua, I tried to keep the Melendez family's status out of everything. I didn't want to be seen as some rich wife tired of not having her way, because I was anything but that. I never wanted money. I never wanted popularity.

The only thing I wanted was a family that understood.

"What do you plan to do if he comes here?" she asked, following me into the house after our trip to the park. Catrina was on her heels, waiting for her promised time with my son.

Those two already adored each other. I could see them staying close as they grew up, no matter how much distance may separate them.

"If he wants me to go back, I most likely will. I just don't want to leave you two," I answered. "I won't leave right away, because with a baby, it's just not that simple."

"Oh, don't worry about me and Cat," Krissy said with a wave of her hand. "I've always wanted to visit Vegas, so you can guarantee that I'll be showing up at your doorstep this summer. Then I can gamble, and get a private tour of it all! If that family of yours owns most of it, I certainly would be taking advantage of it all."

I laughed lightly. I knew she wanted to travel. Krissy only had her parents and a few friends here. She didn't have much really holding her here, so I could see her moving.

Plus, Vegas wasn't all that far away in reality.

"You can't leave, Vidie!" Catrina said. "Friends don't leave."

"I won't be leaving for a little while," I said,

soothing her. "But my family lives in a different place and I'd like to be closer to them if I can. But you know what? I can always call, and we can meet up every few months to see each other."

"Okay," she sighed. "That would have to work, I guess." She tossed her head back at the end of her words, like it was the only option.

"We'll visit," Krissy promised. "And who knows. Maybe we'll just stay there forever one day."

"That I like!" Catrina said happily.

Ah, the simple minds of children. I wish things could be that simple for me.

"Anyway, what do you need me to do? I'm at your beck and call," Krissy said, opening her arms wide.

"Nothing," I laughed. "I need to do some laundry, since Josh thinks peeing on me and himself every time I change his diaper is the best thing."

Krissy laughed out loud at my words. I wasn't kidding, either. I think I did three times the amount of laundry these days.

"That's just gross," Catrina said, shaking her head and turning to my son. "Don't be peeing your clothes. It's just disgusting."

"You're telling me," I breathed out.

The exploding diapers weren't that great either.

**~oOo~**

Two A.M.

I was not a fan of this time of the morning.

It was quiet out in the world. There was no traffic, no one going about their day.

Oh, no. Two in the morning was the time that Joshua had found to be the most awake out of any other time. He refused to go to sleep. Every single night so far.

So, yeah. I wasn't a fan of nighttime wakefulness. Not many people were, either.

Even though I wasn't a fan of this time of night, I did cherish each moment with my son. I watched how he began to wiggle and make a few sounds, looking around for anything his eyes could get on. I loved him more than anything else. He was my world.

I could see so much of Zachariah in him, though. I wasn't sure what Zach would think, but this baby right here had his dark hair. I knew that Josh would be a very handsome man when he grew up, and I couldn't wait to watch all of his firsts. It didn't matter to me if Zach would be there or not. All that mattered was that my son would know he was loved and adored by all of family he knew. Everything else would work itself out in time.

I was prepared, as much as I possibly could be, for whatever my husband would want to do. If he didn't want children, I was okay with that. Joshua and myself were now a packaged deal. It was either both of us, or neither of us.

I wouldn't let him try to change my mind. Zachariah's family would stick behind me one hundred percent.

So now, it was all in his hands.

Zachariah knew my location, and he could come find me himself whenever he was ready for us.

## Chapter 24

### Zachariah

For the next two days, I followed Avidya. I followed her to the store, the park, and even to the post office once with a box of something that was being mailed out. I stayed out of sight, not that she seemed to know, nor think, she was being followed.

Avidya had hardly changed from the girl I fell in love with. I was still trying to process the idea that she had a child.

My child.

I knew that was why she left. I just couldn't figure out why. For so long? And alone? Did she fear what I would do as I had told her I would if she told me she was pregnant? Was that why she ran?

I know I said things that I may not have meant, but surely Avidya would have would have told me. She should have given me a chance.

I wasn't thrilled with my family at the moment, since they had kept this huge secret from me for a full nine months. I had no idea how everyone kept it from me. Would they have continued to do so for years?

It was something I wouldn't put past them.

My father was a master at keeping secrets, but anyone else would have surely told me. Or maybe I just hadn't picked up on the fact that clues were dropped all along the way.

When I called Melio this morning, since he was the only one of my family members I was willing to talk to without blowing up, I told him to let everyone know I'd be back sometime soon. They probably would know where I went to, and none of them would do a thing to stop me now. Not if they knew what was right.

It was bad enough that they hid behind their secrets, all because they thought it was the best thing to do at the time. I knew I'd have a few choice words with all of them when I got back. That could be counted on.

Now, I just had to figure out how to announce my presence to my wife. I had no idea how she'd take it. Would she ignore me?

I wouldn't allow that to happen. She was welcome to try, but I would not be leaving without her. I'd face her, toe to toe, to make sure that she knew that I loved her more than life, and that I couldn't live without her.

I couldn't return without her beside me. I couldn't fucking live without her, and she had to see that.

She couldn't stay here, and I couldn't leave her.

I knew there would be a few choice words between us, most likely more on my part than anything else. I would get my say in, and she better listen to me when I did. I'd tie her to a chair to make her listen if it came to that.

When Travis called on his way back just a week ago, I wasn't sure what I would be finding here. I didn't know for sure what made him even come here at first. Now I understood. Everything became clear now.

Still didn't change my anger and the situation, though. Nothing would.

*"Keep an open mind,"* he stated over the phone. *"And don't jump to conclusions."*

*Yeah right.*

*"How long has she been there?"* I asked after he gave me the town name. I knew he had known where my wife went to for months, and just now told me her location. A few months too late in my opinion.

*"Long enough,"* he answered. *"So you can't just go in and drag her away. People would notice if she just up and left without a word."*

*"Who says I'd do that?"* I huffed, running a hand down my face.

*"I know you,"* Travis laughed in a mumbled way.

*"Who even knows if she wants to come back to that kind of life. She's not the same girl from a year ago. She knows what she wants, and she'll stop at nothing to make sure she gets to keep what she's worked so hard to achieve."*

*He paused, thinking about how to say what he needed to get out. I wanted to demand answers to so many questions.*

*"I know you want her back with you, by your side. She should be, but give her a chance to explain her side of things. She deserves a choice in her life. And this one you cannot take away again. She'd hate you if you tried to do that and force her to go back with you."*

*"As long as she'll listen to me, too," I sighed. I knew he was right; didn't mean I had to like it.*

*"She likes to hang out at the main park on nice sunny days with a friend. She won't be hard to find," Travis said before ending the call.*

Avidya wasn't hard to find, just like Travis had stated. It was almost too easy. That made me question myself was if I should have come sooner. Should I have demanded to know her location sooner?

Wait.

I did demand to know. Constantly.

No one told me anything!

Therefore, for two days, I followed her. Maybe I did it for my own selfish reasons. Maybe I did it because I had to make sure that no other man was in her life.

Whatever the reason, I followed her. I followed her until I had had an idea about what to do.

I was still unsure of how to go about it, even as I sat on the front step, waiting for her to appear. My elbows were braced on the top of my knees as I waited. I knew it was only a few more minutes before she would come home as I had left the park as Avidya buckled our baby into the car. I knew it would give me enough time to gather my mental strength to face my wife.

It was maybe ten minutes later when the redhaired woman pulled up to the house next door. I kept my head down in my hands as I heard the car doors open and then close.

"Will you be okay?" I heard the redhead say, her concerned voice carrying my way.

I didn't catch a reply, but I assumed that Avidya nodded or gave some sort of acknowledgement. A few moments later, I heard soft, light footsteps coming my way. I kept my posture, hiding my face and fears.

What did I have to fear?

Everything.

"Zachariah," Avidya sighed, her voice just above a whisper. She didn't sound surprised to see me here. She didn't seem happy, either. She almost sounded like she expected me to be here.

"Hello," I said, raising my head to see her. She stood maybe a yard away from me with the baby carrier on one arm and what I assumed was a diaper bag in the other. Today, her hair was down past her shoulders with the tips slightly curled. Her green eyes were bright with life, yet tired at the same time.

She stood there, seeming not to know what to say. I could relate. I had so many things I had thought I'd be saying by now, but none of that was coming to mind. I just wanted to pull her into a hug and never let her go.

Screw talking. Screw trying to win my way back into her life.

I just wanted to stare at her forever. She was my sun, my life. She hadn't changed one bit

"Are you two just going to stare at each other, or are you going to actually talk?" called the neighbor as she made her way to us. "My God!" Her steps grew harder, in a stomping sort of way, as she neared.

"Krissy," Avidya sighed in warning.

"Don't," she barked, turning her blazing eyes to me.

"You lay one hand on this girl, and I'll make your life a living hell, got it?"

"Got it," I appeased her. I would say that I'd never do such a thing, but yeah, that wouldn't help matters.

"Don't go yelling at her, either," she went on, placing her hands on her hips as she gave me what would be called a 'mother look.' "And no dragging her away. You do anything to make her cry, I'll cut you."

"Krissy," Avidya hissed. "I'll be fine. Now go."

"I'll be back in an hour," she stated before flipping around and marching back to her house.

"Sorry," Avidya said with a shrug. "She means well."

"She should," I said, still not moving from where I sat. "I'll behave. I just...we need to talk."

She nodded as she stepped up beside me, setting down the car seat and unlocking the door. Once the door was opened, she picked up the seat and walked in, calling behind her, "Come on in."

I pushed myself up and entered the house. At first glance, it fit Avidya to a T. Hardly anything personal, but the coloring and simplicity of it all was entirely her.

It even smelled like her to an extent.

"Make yourself at home," she said, placing the seat

on the table and bag next to it. She then started to get the baby out of the seat. I could hear him, or her, grunt as she removed him from the contraption.

I took a seat on the edge of the couch, not sure where to sit, or even what to say now that I knew she wasn't going to run screaming. I felt out of my element more than ever.

This was not what I was expecting. It completely threw me off.

"I'm surprised," she mused as she held the baby to her chest, patting its butt. "I've expected you to show up for weeks. Figured you must have forgotten all about me."

"I could never forget you," I said quietly with a shake of my head. "No one told me anything until recently."

"I'm sure you know why by now," she stated, taking a seat farthest from me as possible. My heart hurt at that. I wanted her as close as possible, but understood her need for space. I was sure that once I touched her, even a simple touch, I wouldn't be able to keep my hands to myself.

I already didn't want to keep my hands to myself. Motherhood suited her very well.

Something I was not expecting.

"For so long, I wasn't sure. I couldn't figure out why you would leave me just like that. Without any warning or any explanation. There was no word from you at all," I stated, my voice growing colder with each word that passed my lips. "I...I didn't know what to do. Why would you just fucking leave, Avidya? Why?"

"You once said you'd take the choice away from me if I were to end up pregnant," she said. How could her voice be so calm at this? Had she been thinking about what to say all along if I happened to show up on her doorstep just as I had? "I couldn't risk it. I couldn't just sit back and let you kill my child because you didn't want to be a father. So I did the only thing I could do."

"So you just left? Just like that? You could have just talked to me about it. I would have listened!" I nearly yelled. I stood up in my fit of anger, running my hands over my face.

"I knew you wouldn't listen if I even tried, Zach," she said with a sad shake of her head. "I saw how you froze up at the mention of any child that we would have ever had. That right there gave me all the information I needed. I didn't have a choice. Not when it came to what I want out of life."

"You did!" I seethed, slapping my hands against my

legs. "You had every choice you ever needed."

"Not when it came to this," she stated without a beat. "That choice was taken away. Everyone knew that having a child was not in your plans. Even your own parents knew that!"

"Is it even mine?" I huffed out. As the words passed my lips, I regretted them. I saw how Avidya's face paled at my question and I wanted to die for even asking such a shitty thing.

"How could you even ask me something like that?" Avidya asked, appalled. "Of course, he's yours."

I was a total dick. I knew I shouldn't be saying things out of anger, as it was what got us into such a situation to begin with.

"If the only reason you showed up was to insult me like that, you may as well go back," she went on, pointing at the door in the process. "I will never let you talk to me like that. Nor to *our* son. That right there is another reason why I left."

"Oh? You have a list of reasons?" I asked on a laugh.

"Do I need a list?" she responded, her voice hard and cold. "It's bad enough you hate children. It's sick that you wanted me to have an abortion. It was horrible that I had to leave you so I could keep the one thing I ever wanted."

"I gave you everything you asked for," I said, my voice hard to match hers.

"I never asked for anything but to keep a child that we made," she stated in fury. "It was the only thing I wanted, and you had it all planned out. You already knew what you would do to make sure no baby would be born from my body."

As her voice rose in volume, the baby she still held began to cry and squirm in her arms. His cry turned into more of a demanding wail by the second and Avidya's burning glare could have made me a pile of ashes right where I sat.

I deserved her anger and much more. I hadn't come here to fight with her, only to prove that I could be the man that I wanted to be.

I had my work cut out for me, and now I wasn't so sure I would get my wife back.

## Chapter 25

### Zachariah

I knew that walking into the life that Avidya had here would be hard. I just hadn't thought it would be so hard to talk to her. My emotions were everywhere. I wanted to yell, kiss, and spank her all at once. None of which were possible right now.

I was great at putting my foot in my mouth. The words just came out all on their own, and it was too late to take them back.

The screaming baby didn't help matters. I just wanted to get this over with and start on living again with this girl that held my heart.

I kept my mouth shut as Avidya tended to the baby. I watched how she managed to soothe him with a bottle and diaper change. It seemed so easy to do so, yet I was still left baffled.

How could I not want children when I saw my wife giving loving care to one? She was pro at it. Maybe I shouldn't have jumped to the conclusion that I never wanted a child and given her desire a thought. Maybe I should have let her do what she wanted. Heck, maybe I was at the entire fault here.

Maybes never went anywhere.

So, I sat there and watched. And waited.

From here on out, I had to tread carefully with anything and everything I would do. I had to be mindful of what I would say, knowing it could either make us or break us. I hated the idea that I could lose this—this that was right in front of me—because of my stupid words. Stupid words that were said but not meant.

If only I could move on past this. If only we could both just skip all these and have our happily ever after.

If only life would work that way.

"How old?" I asked towards the baby that was now calmed down.

"Six weeks today," she answered. "He arrived eight weeks too early, but he's healthy and alive."

"Why?" I couldn't help but ask.

"I assume he wanted out," she laughed sadly. "It didn't help matters when I was held at gunpoint and forced to watch my family get shot right in front of me. Right here where I am standing now, actually."

"Who would do that?" I asked, fear consuming me. My wife had been in danger, and I was nowhere near here to help keep her safe. My heart thumped in my chest, but felt like my entire body was on alert now that I knew what danger Avidya was in.

All this could have been avoided if she'd have stayed.

Looking around the room, I couldn't tell that someone had been killed inside this house. No wonder why Travis had come here and didn't tell me right away what was up. I would have taken a jet and been here within minutes if I had known.

"Aaron," she answered easily. How the fuck could she be so calm about that?

"How did he come here?" I asked, leaning forward.

"I'm assuming he drove," she said, rolling her eyes. "I didn't ask."

*Really? Did she have to joke about this?* I thought to myself.

"That's not what I meant," I said through clenched teeth. I was trying really hard to calm my anger, and she was not helping me at all.

"He came here to get me. He wanted to use me to get money and who knows what else. He was one sick twisted man who needed mental help," she answered. "I think he was bipolar, or at least something along the lines of that."

"Where is he now?" I seethed, anger and fear clouding my vision. I wanted to kill that fucker ten times over. I had thought he was still at the rundown, druggy apartment complex he had been keeping to since his reappearance a year or so ago. I thought he was so high on dope, he'd never come looking for Avidya without leaving a blazing trail behind him.

"Wherever the men took him," she said, looking me dead in the eye. "I was in a bit of shock, so I didn't really pay attention to what Travis had barked out. And I don't really want to know. As long as he's dead and stays that way, who really cares?"

"Did he touch you?" I asked slowly.

"No," she said, shaking her head. "He tied Taylor to a chair after somehow knocking him out, but he never touched me. I called Kent, and he sent men here to take care of him."

"Good," I said, my voice hard. "I should have put a bullet in his head years ago."

"That's already been done," she huffed out as she walked to the baby swing and put the baby into it before starting it so it swung from side to side in a slow motion.

"Good. Saves me the trouble," I said, letting my body relax as I knew there was no longer a threat. "Did he say anything about why he wanted both of us dead?"

"No," she answered, turning to face me once more. "I didn't want to ask, either. I couldn't risk my life."

"Are *you* okay?" I asked.

"As well as I can be," she said.

Surely, she knew that was not the answer I was looking for. Wisely, I didn't push.

"Alright, are we just going to not say what needs to be said? Because if so, you can just leave now. Save us the trouble," she said, folding her arms across her chest.

"Avidya," I sighed. "I'd rather do much more than just talking. But I don't want to step over this line we have here between us. I don't even know where to start. I want to know so many things, but where do I even start? Where would it be best to start without making you upset at me more than you already are? I screwed up, and I want to fix it. I just don't know *how*. My entire family knows why you left, and no one told me shit about it! So how am I supposed to pretend what we had wasn't a lie?"

"You know the reason why I left," she stated calmly.

"Not entirely, no," I said, trying to figure her out.

"Think back to that double date with Travis and Kenna," she said.

Yeah, I could remember that. I wouldn't call it a date with how it turned out. Avidya had called *red* at the end, killing anything I had been trying to achieve. All I wanted for her was to see how Travis and Kenna were able get along so well with their type of relationship. They were happy, and I wanted nothing more than that for Avidya and myself.

I gave her a nod.

"Do you know the reason I called it all to stop?" she asked.

"We didn't ever really talk about it," I said. "It was only a couple of days before you upped and left. So no. I don't know why you called it off. Everything. Not just that night, but everything."

Before she replied, she took a seat on the couch, as far away from me as possible once more. She took a moment to gather her thoughts before going forward. She was the type of girl that always said what was on her mind—that hadn't changed.

It was one of many things that I loved about her.

"You said you'd force me to have an abortion. You didn't even listen to Kenna as she tried to make you see how much that thought hurt me," she went on, her voice quiet. She looked down at the floor as she spoke, "That night…that night I knew I had no choice. I knew I was pregnant, Zach. And you clearly weren't going to change your decision. You weren't going to change that choice about taking away the only thing I wanted besides you."

"So you just ran?" I asked, shocked. How could she hide this from me for so long?

"Yes," she said, forcing back tears. "If I didn't run, I would have told you. I'd have told you and you'd make me get rid of him."

"I'd have listened," I said, knowing the words were a lie as I said them.

If I hadn't felt like shit before, I sure did now.

"No. No you wouldn't," she said with a sad laugh. "I know you well enough. Or at least I did. I saw it that night that you would never see reason. It broke my heart to leave, but I had no other choice. If I wanted to keep that little baby over there alive, and safe, I had to leave. I did what I had to do to make sure of that. I had to make sure you didn't take him, and I will do everything to make sure you can't."

"Avidya," I sighed, putting my head in my hands.

Was there any way I could fix this? Would she be able to forgive me?

## Chapter 26

### Avidya

Why did he have to make this so hard? Was he really stupid enough to think that he had done nothing to cause me to leave? Did he think that I left because of something that had nothing to do with him? What was I to do?

"I'm sorry," Zachariah finally sighed out after a few silent moments.

"Yeah, that's not going to cut it," I replied. A simple sorry was not going to be enough. Not by a long shot.

"What can I do? I want to fix *us*. Please," he said, nearly begging.

I couldn't say anything. I had no idea what to say to that. For most people, saying they needed time was what would sometimes fix this. But time was not on our side. We had nine months' worth of time, there was no more time to be needed.

"I don't know," I said. "I don't know if there can be an *us* anymore." There was no chance of us getting back together if he could only be angry at my choices. I would never willingly live with another person that thought they had complete control over me like my parents had.

"Is there someone else?" he asked, sounding scared that there was a possibility of that.

"No," I huffed through my nose. "There's only been you." How could he even ask that of me?

"So why? Why can't you just let me in?" he asked. His voice rose a pitch at the end of his question.

"It's not that easy," I said, doing my best to keep my voice down. "You hurt me, Zach. You hurt me so much because you wouldn't let me have a baby. You have no idea how much that hurt me inside."

"I didn't even know you had one until two days ago!" he seethed, slapping his hands on his knees. "God. I can't have a chance to even think about it, or about the what ifs when you won't let me have a chance to even grasp the concept that you have a child. And you *hid* it from me."

"You can't pull that on me," I said hotly. "If you had known, what would you have done?"

He remained quiet, giving me what I needed in answer. I knew exactly what he would have done.

"See," I said. "You proved my point. You can't blame me for leaving."

"I didn't say I did," he said. "Doesn't change that you left me. You think I hurt you. But you hurt me, too. You broke my heart. You left me. You left us all without a word. That letter you left did nothing to help. You fucking broke me, Avidya."

Near the end of the words, his voice finally broke. That tiny break in his voice caused my tears to finally fall. After that first tear fell, there was nothing I could do to stop the rest. There was no way I could as my body shook with each passing minute.

As sobs racked me, his arms wrapped around me and pulled me into him. I never thought I'd be able to feel his warmth again. I never thought I'd be able to feel his arms around me.

"God, I'm so sorry, Vidie," he whispered in my ear. "I'm sorry. I wish I could turn back time."

I was unable to reply, knowing if I opened my mouth, I wouldn't be able to make any coherent words.

Instead, I let him hold me. I let him comfort me. I let him do what I had wanted so long.

I just wanted to be held. I wanted to have his arms around me for so long, I hadn't thought it would be possible to have them again. Taylor never hugged me. Krissy had a time or two, but nothing like this. Nothing else felt like Zachariah's arms around me.

Being in his arms made things seem a bit better. Maybe we could have a chance at fixing what was broken. It would take a while, that was for sure. But maybe we could be happy together.

I don't know how long I let him hold me as sobs wracked my body. I don't know how much time passed as I shed tear after tear, soaking his shirt. As I slowly calmed, I still let his arms stay wrapped around me.

Joshua began to grunt, causing me to pull away from Zachariah with a sniff.

"Sorry," I said, wiping my tears away.

"You have nothing to be sorry about," he said, brushing my hair away from my face. "I should be the one that is sorry. Not you."

I gave him a tight smile as the grunts turned into cries.

After getting Joshua's diaper changed, I asked one of the many things I feared to know the answer too. But if we were going to move beyond this, I had to take the step to do it. He didn't seem to know how.

"Do you want to hold him?" I asked.

"What?" he said, eyes widening.

"Hold him?" I repeated. After a moment with no

answer I let out a breath. Why had I even tried? I knew I couldn't expect a huge turn-about like that. I had to take this all one step at a time.

I held Joshua on in one arm while I readied a bottle with my other. After a week of practice, I thought I was getting it all down. The tiredness was something I had yet to get the hang of. But it was all part of being a parent.

Once I was back on the couch, I couldn't stop the yawn that escaped.

"Who's Taylor?" he asked after I got situated. He seemed afraid to know for sure who the man that had lived here was.

"Was my uncle," I said, not taking my eyes off the baby in my arms.

"Was?" he repeated.

"Aaron killed him when Taylor stabbed him. He tried to save me," I answered quietly.

"Oh," he said. That simple two letter word.

"Tell me what you've been doing here," he said, leaning against the back of the couch.

"Why?" I asked.

"So I can maybe understand," he shrugged.

With a deep breath, I began to tell him. I told him how I feared my life, the life of Josh. I told him that I came here to do anything I could to keep my baby. I spoke the words as though nothing had been different. I said each word as though it was my last. I let my words be filled with heartache and peace with my choices.

I let my words tell what I felt every single day I lived without him by my side. I told him that I hated the idea of leaving. I told him that I did the only thing I could to keep on living.

I told him I was alive only because of the life I had given.

And nothing would change that.

Ever.

"You can't take him from me, if that's why you are here now. I won't let you," I said towards the man I loved. After everything, I still loved him as much as I ever had before. "If it comes between the two of you, you won't ever win, Zach. I left to keep him, and I'd do it again."

"You won't," he said. "I won't take him, and you don't have to leave again. I'll do whatever you want. Just please, give me another chance."

Could I give him a chance? I wanted to. He was here now, after so many months. He was here listening to my words instead of trying to talk over them.

So maybe, just maybe, I could.

## Chapter 27

### Zachariah

Was I doing the right thing? I had no idea. As the words passed my lips, I knew they were true.

We were both hurting. We were both in need of something from each other. We couldn't live without one another, and I'd do anything to get both of us to be on the same page, or at least as close as possible. I'd take her back in a heartbeat, the child too. I'd just deal with it, and hope that I could come to terms with everything.

Hopefully.

I could pretend that the child was never there if I had too. I wasn't sure if I wanted to be a father, but I could deal with it being in my house. For Avidya, I would.

As Avidya told me what her life had been like the past months had been like for her. I listened to each and every single word that passed her lips. I hung onto them as if my life depended on them. I listened to everything she had to say. Although she hardly looked my way, I could see the sadness on her face.

She really was as sad as I had been. At least she had a reason to keep on living, and try to make something here.

She did a better job of everything compared to how I had been handling my life. I would have easily spent every moment drunk if I could have.

I was angry that she had to face Aaron and that everyone had known all the reasons she left me. I wasn't sure how my family was able to keep it from me for so long.

She knew how to handle the baby, even after a long NICU stay. I felt horrible that she had to deal with all of this alone. Why didn't she call me? Why didn't she ask for help? Surely, she needed someone more than just the girl next door to help her.

"Why didn't you call?" I asked, not able to hold the question any longer. It should have been so easy for her to pick up that phone and call me. I would have answered, no matter what time of day or night it was.

"I wanted to," she sighed tiredly. "There were a few times I was so close to picking up the phone to call you. I knew your voice would help me make it through the tough days. There were so many days I almost couldn't keep on going. But I knew you would be able to hear that something was wrong and you'd want to know. I would have told you, too. I needed someone to be here to help, to listen. Sure, I had Krissy and Travis, but they weren't *you.*"

"I'd have come earlier if I'd known," I said. "If you would have told me . . ."

"I was afraid of what you would do," she said quietly as though she was afraid to say the words, or maybe afraid of my reaction. Or both. "I figured that Travis would have told you sooner though. He had to know that I needed my husband to be here to help soothe my worries and stress."

"He didn't tell me anything until he was on the way back home," I answered. "He was at least half way back by the time he called."

"He almost didn't go back," she stated. "But I knew he missed Kenna and needed to go back eventually. I told him I could handle this on my own. And I want to think that I am."

"It looks like you are a pro to me," I shrugged.

"I'm doing the best that I can," she stated. "It's not as easy as it looks. But I didn't expect it to be all that easy. The lack of sleep isn't the most exciting thing to deal with."

I didn't know what to say to that. I had nothing to say, since I didn't even know the first thing about parenting. The lack of sleep, that I could relate to.

"So, how long do you plan to stay?" she asked after a thick silent moment.

"I'm not sure," I answered. What I didn't say was that I'd be here until I won her heart back. I'd do whatever I had to do to prove it. To prove that I wanted her. To prove that I still loved her more than anything else. She was my life.

"Okay," she said on a sigh of defeat.

Was she upset I may not stay long, or was she upset because I may never leave?

"I'll stay as long as you'd like me to," I whispered, looking at her. Although she didn't look at me, my eyes begged her to understand that I wouldn't leave her until she asked me to.

"I'm sure you have things that you need to do," she said, refusing to meet my eyes.

"You are more important right now," I said. "Anything that I left behind can wait."

"I'm no one," she said on a sniff.

"You are Avidya Melendez," I said after scooting over right beside her. "You are my wife. You are a mother, and you are part of a huge family that will do anything to make you happy."

She simply gave me a watery smile before leaning her head against my shoulder.

"I'm just Avidya." The muttered words went

straight to my heart.

She was so much more, and it would be just one more thing I'd prove to her.

## Chapter 28

### Avidya

After laying Joshua down in the bassinet that Krissy was letting me borrow, I decided to go take a shower. I wasn't sure when I'd get another chance to get one with Josh's random feedings. Normally, I'd asked Krissy to sit and keep an eye on the baby for me so I could get a fast one in, but with Zachariah I thought I'd be okay to get one.

"Knock on the door if he wakes up please," I said before hopping into the shower. Once he gave me a nod, I shut the door.

Once the almost too warm water hit my back, I let more tears fall.

Why me? Why was it always me?

I didn't know what to do any more. I wanted so badly to let Zach take away all my problems. I wanted him to stand up and be the father I desperately wanted. I just wanted things that were now so far out of reach, I had no choice but to put them aside.

As I told Zach, I was just me. Just the girl that always had to fight her way through each passing day because of one thing or another.

I was just *tired* of everything.

I had thought I could do this all on my own, but the past week with very little sleep had certainly showed me just how hard this parenting thing was. Actually, it'd been longer than just a week of very little sleep. I had hardly gotten much since I gave birth to my little boy who I loved more than anything. It was also that same time I lost one of my last living blood relatives.

Most people would call it post-partum depression, but I called it dealing. And I was dealing with it all as well as I could.

The thought of going back to the family that I left was a very close possibility. I knew if I went back, it'd have been so easy to have the help, the love, and the support that I needed. If I did, I feared that Zachariah would have done something to take my child away.

I didn't know this man any more. Nine months of being away from each other, I had no way of knowing if he'd do something stupid. I had no way of knowing if he'd take what I was so determined to keep.

So, I knew I had to stay strong and keep to my plan and keep things as they were.

The only way I'd move back to the one place that felt like home was if he was able to show me that he could be the father to this child. If Zachariah could show me that we were something that I did have to give up in the end, then I'd return.

If only things would turn out to be happily ever after.

By the time I got out of the shower and dressed, I felt more tired than I had before taking the shower. I wanted nothing but to go try to take a quick nap before Joshua woke up again, since he was a demanding little thing.

When I went back to the living room, I found Zachariah staring at our son as he slept in the bassinet next to the couch where I had moved it. I wasn't expecting anything out of ten minutes.

I hoped that Zachariah would be open to the idea of all this, but I was not going to hold my breath for it. I knew his feelings on this subject, and I wasn't going to push it.

He had to know by now that Joshua and I were a package deal.

"Good shower?" he asked as he spotted me.

"Sure," I said, tight lipped.

"What can I do?" he asked after a moment.

I blinked at him. There was nothing he could do. Nothing that could help ease the hurt that panged inside of my chest.

"Nothing," I muttered, flopping down a bit too hard on the couch.

"You need sleep," he said, looking at me like he knew just how tired I was. I wanted to sleep. I wanted to be held. I want to let my husband hold me and make the entire world disappear.

"You're telling me," I yawned out. "You try going weeks without much sleep and let me know how you feel."

"I'll wisely keep my mouth closed to that comment," he sighed. "Go lay down, Avidya."

"Can't," I said, letting my eyes slide closed.

"Why not?" he asked, confused. "I'll...I'll watch him."

"Do you even know how to change a diaper? Make a bottle?" I asked, opening my eyes to a slit to look his way.

"Kinda," he shrugged. "I'll make due."

I wasn't so sure about the idea of him taking care of the baby. Would he really be able to? Would he do something to make me regret ever letting him into the house?

"I promise I won't leave or do anything stupid," he said, knowing what I was thinking. "I promise, Avidya."

After a moment of thought, I moved to where my head rested on the armrest, my legs pulled up so I wasn't touching Zach. Of course, that didn't last long. He took my feet into his lap, his warm hands soothing me as I let my eyes slid closed.

I was out in seconds.

~oOo~

I had been so used to only getting a few minutes of sleep here and there. Maybe half an hour if I was lucky. I knew I slept at least a couple of hours before I woke in a panic. I hadn't heard the baby. I hadn't heard Zach move or make a sound.

I couldn't help but wake up in blind panic. Any parent would do the same.

Opening my eyes and sitting up on the couch, I looked around and found the living room to be empty. The blanket that I assumed Zach covered me with was bunched in my lap.

Where were they? He didn't take off with my baby, did he?

He couldn't.

My heart pounded in my chest, way too fast as my

breathing grew heavy. Right as I was about go into a full out panic, the front door was pushed open. Zachariah and Krissy stepped inside.

"Feeling better?" Zachariah asked me.

I nodded, afraid to say anything.

My shoulders relaxed as Krissy handed Joshua to me, most likely knowing I was on the verge of panic.

"He was poopy," Zach explained. "I didn't want to wake you up, so I asked her…"

"He couldn't handle the smell," Krissy laughed. "So he came over for my help."

I looked between the two, seeing that Zachariah wasn't too thrilled about having to ask for help.

I couldn't help but laugh as I put the baby up to my chest. It was the type of laugh that I hadn't had for a very long time.

"Glad it amuses you," he grunted with a smile on his lips.

"He did well. He even made a couple of bottles," Krissy said. "He's a keeper."

I gave her a smile, hoping she was right.

Just maybe we would be okay.

## Chapter 29

## Zachariah

Somehow, I was able to keep my emotions from showing as I promised Avidya that I could handle watching the kid for a little bit. She looked so tired, and I wanted to do something, anything, to help her. I knew she wouldn't ask. She was too strong willed to do that.

I couldn't help but tell her to just go to sleep. I promised I'd take care of the baby so she could get some sleep. I could handle it.

I hoped.

I did well after I put a blanket over Avidya. It hadn't taken all that long for her to fall asleep. I felt horrible that she had been through so much in such a short amount of time. I knew she had been through just as much stress as I had been, if not more.

At least I knew I had people who would keep my back if I got into trouble. I had a family I could always talk to. I had a place to live my life. I didn't have to worry losing everything in a heartbeat.

With Avidya, she had lost both parents, a place to live, and her entire life. She willingly gave up having people on her side to keep her baby. She left me to keep this little human being that I wanted nothing to do with.

She had given up more than I would have been able to. Yet, here she was still on living.

Avidya was so much stronger than I gave her credit for.

When Joshua began to squirm, I was quick to pick him up and get a bottle made. I didn't want his cries to wake up his sleeping mother if I could help it. It wasn't all that hard to figure out how to make a bottle, or change a wet diaper. I watched enough TV to know how to do it all. At least I had the thought of how to do it down.

It was easier to watch than actually do it, but I did get the diaper changed and bottle made. This little baby was a wiggly little thing.

What I wasn't counting on, or even expecting, was the feeling I got when I held Joshua in my arms. He was so small in the huge world. He had no one but his mother to care for him, and he didn't even know what life outside of being a baby was like. He just wanted love, food, and to be cared for.

He didn't have many wants. He had nothing to worry about. He had no one he would ever worry about letting down.

I wasn't expecting my heart to grow, giving it room to maybe love this little one.

He looked so much like Avidya, it was scary, but I could also see myself in him.

What would he be like as a grown man? Would he be taking my spot in the family business? Would he be one of the men that I bossed around?

I could never do that. I didn't want this baby to grow up to be a man like that. I didn't want him anywhere near what I did. Would there be a chance he could live outside of all that? Or would he be forced into it because he thought it was the cool thing to do, just like I had at one time.

There were so many new worries now. The worries I never thought I'd be able to have because I didn't want a child.

I had a child. A son. One that would no doubt follow in my footsteps.

A son that I was now fully in love with.

I never thought that someone could fall in love with something so fast. I hadn't thought it was possible when I found Avidya, and I didn't think for once second it would happen with this child. But I was proven wrong as I held Joshua against my chest and breathed in his baby scent.

At that moment, I promised myself I'd do anything to protect this little one from that type of world. I'd do anything in my power to keep my life out of his. I would do anything to make sure he didn't have to be a man in the family business.

It was the least I could do.

Now, facing Avidya would not be so easy. I knew she thought I would be leaving him, leaving her. I had news for her—I was not going to leave. Even if she told me to, I would not be going anywhere.

Ever.

When Joshua began to grunt and fart, I knew I was facing something I had no idea how to handle. There was no way I wanted to wake Avidya up to change a diaper, so I went next door, asking for help. Another thing I never saw myself ever doing.

Krissy made fun of me, but was quick to do what I was too chicken to do.

When I went back to the house, Avidya was awake in panic, and I felt horrible that she felt like I'd do something to either one of them.

I felt out of the loop as I retook my seat on the couch as Krissy busied herself with cleaning up the small mess I made in the kitchen from making the bottles.

"Thanks," Avidya said my way.

"Of course," I stated. "You needed sleep."

"Did you two talk?" Krissy asked, facing both of us with her arms across her chest.

"I guess so," Avidya said.

"That doesn't sound all that promising," Krissy stated on a huff.

"We still have more to talk about," I said. "A lot. And I won't be leaving until everything is cleared up."

"Then you'll just leave, right? After everything is cleared up, you'll leave and then what?" Avidya said, glaring at the wall in front of her.

"No," I said, my voice quiet. "I won't leave. Not until you tell me to. And even then, I won't be leaving without you and our son, Avidya."

"Why?" she asked, her voice filled with tears. "You got what you came for, didn't you? Why would you want me now? You don't want kids."

"Why?" I asked. "Because I love you, Avidya. You are my life. My everything. I can't live without you. I understand the reason why you ran. I can't hold you hostage because you felt the need to save your baby. I won't hold that against you ever.

"I won't leave without you. I love you, Avidya. And

I love Joshua just as much. We will have a family that you want, and I'll do whatever it takes to show you that. I won't go back until you will go back with me. If you don't ever want to go back, then I'll move here. I'll leave everything behind.

"*You* and Joshua are what matters more than anything else in this world. You are my life, my world. I can't go back to living life like I had the past nine months. I refuse to. You are what I want, Avidya. And nothing will change that."

"Kiss," Krissy whispered with a bounce.

"No," Avidya laughed, a happy laugh this time.

"I wouldn't be opposed to that," I stated, lifting an eyebrow.

"Kissing leads to other things," she said, giving me that knowing look. "And I can't do that yet."

"So?" Krissy laughed. "Who cares. Just kiss and make up."

"Krissy," Avidya said, a smile in her voice. "Thanks, but no thanks, on the advice."

"Find, whatever," Krissy said with an eyeroll. "You both need some food. I'll leave you two be, but if you need me, you know where to find me."

That, we certainly both did know.

"Is she always so bossy and demanding?" I asked as Krissy shut the door behind her.

"Oh, that was nothing," Avidya laughed. "Just wait until you see how she acts around her daughter. It gets worse."

I couldn't help but look at my wife, letting a smile pull against my lips. She was amazing in all ways possible.

## Chapter 30

## Avidya

After ordering pizza, Josh was in his bassinet, Zachariah and I sat on the couch, just enjoying each other's company. The TV on some channel that neither one of us paid attention to.

It felt comfortable to sit here by his side with his arm wrapped around me. My head leaned against his shoulder as all the stresses of the world left me.

I never wanted to move. I never wanted to change things again. I had given up so much for my own personal gain, and it seemed that he understood. He didn't hold it against me. He didn't use it as leverage.

He was just the same Zachariah that I had fallen in love with. The same man that I never knew what to expect when it came to new things.

Maybe he really could be the father I had hoped for him to turn out to be. I knew it wouldn't be a sudden thing, but he would be a dad. He'd be okay.

*We'd* be okay.

"Do we have a chance?" I asked, not taking my eyes off the TV, fearing his reaction.

"A chance at what?" he asked, confused.

"Of being together. Of being happy?" I clarified.

"I think so," he answered after a moment of thought. "If we tried to compromise, we can try to be happy together."

"You comprise?" I laughed. "I don't see that happening.

"It is possible," he grumbled. "If you give me a chance to show that I can."

I had to give him a chance; I knew I had to. It wouldn't be easy, but my heart and soul was his. It always would be. I had to give him a chance to prove to me that we could be happy as a family.

"Alright," I sighed.

"Really?" he asked, surprised I was willing to work with him.

"Yes," I smiled. "I miss everything we had. I miss the family. I miss feeling like I belonged."

"Everyone has missed you," he said. "Even Toby. He's not very happy with me."

"I don't think he ever was," I mused. "That poor boy. He probably was as hurt as you were when I left."

"If he was old enough to drink himself to death, yes," Zachariah agreed. "He thinks I made you leave. And he won't talk to anyone as far as I know."

"I should have left him a letter, too," I mused. "He has to hate me like everyone else."

"No one hates you," he said, his voice firm. "They all knew why you left, or at least had an idea. Toby's just a kid and will understand once he sees you are perfectly fine. Give Violet a call later this week and talk to him. I'm sure everyone would love to hear from you."

"I'm sorry I didn't call you again," I said as sadness hit me once more.

"I can understand, I think," he stated. "It's in the past. Let's just move on from here, okay?"

"Sounds good," I smiled, leaning into him more than I already was. Moving on sounded like the best plan of action. Putting the past back into the past was the best way to move on. We both forgave the other, so we had to keep on moving forward.

**~oOo~**

A few days went by, and between everything, Zachariah and I were able to get in a pretty decent routine. I was still tired, but not nearly as bad as I had been since I was able to get a little bit more sleep. Since the first time that Zachariah held Joshua, he was actually helping me with a feeding once a night.

That alone was showing me that he really was in it all the way. He wasn't going to run off, leaving me or our son to fend for ourselves. Although, if that did happen, I would be able to deal. I wouldn't have a choice.

Krissy made sure to stop by a few times a day. I think it was more of the fact she wanted to make sure he wasn't hurting us. I knew that Zach would never do that, but I didn't mind.

I knew I would be going back home sooner or later. It was all a matter of time. Right now, there was no way that I'd take Joshua anywhere because I didn't think I could handle stopping every few hours to feed and change a diaper. That, and also all of his doctors were here and they knew him. I wouldn't be leaving yet.

Not for another few months at least.

I was sure that Zachariah was itching to get back, but he never said anything. He never acted as though we were a burden that had to be taken care of before he returned.

For once, it felt like we were a family with no worries. For once, we were just us.

After Zachariah hinted again to call someone,

anyone, in the family, I finally did. I talked to Julia enough times, I knew it wasn't her that he was hinting at me to call. No, he wanted me to call his sister.

So, I did after Josh was asleep in his bassinet and Zach was answering one of his calls. He had been making sure to not answer any phone calls unless it was family. Apparently, he was using this as a vacation. Whatever worked, I guess.

Violet answered on the second ring. It was as though she expected me to be calling, which I wouldn't have put it past my husband letting her know.

"Hello, Avidya," she greeted, sounding happy to hear from me.

"Hey, Violet," I replied. "How are you doing?"

"Doing well. You?" she returned.

"Doing better now," I answered. I really was.

"Good," she sighed out. "When will you be back? We all miss you."

"I'm not sure yet," I stated. "I can't come back until late next month, since Joshua has a doctor's appointment that would be best to do here. Depending on that, then maybe that same week."

"That would be good," she said. "How's Zach handling it all?"

"Better than I expected," I answered truthfully. "I figured he'd yell and demand things. But he's been great so far. To the both of us."

"Good," she sighed. "I would hang him by the balls if he wasn't nice."

I barked out a laugh, knowing how true that was. His entire family would have done that and more if Zachariah did anything to harm me, or make me do something I didn't want to do.

"How's Toby doing?" I asked.

"Today isn't too bad of a day," she sighed in answer. "He's been more withdrawn since you left, and we can't get him to really branch out from it at all. He had been talking to Melio, but that hasn't happened for months now. He worries that I'll get rid of him."

"That wouldn't ever happen," I was quick to say.

"Never," she agreed. "But he's...well, he just has to see that won't ever happen."

"Do you think he'd talk to me?" I asked.

"Maybe. He'll at least listen, I think. I'll put on you speaker," Violet said before there was a bit of background noise that indicated she was moving around to find the boy.

After a moment, I could hear Violet explaining to Toby that I was on the phone and wanted to talk to him.

Taking that was my go ahead, I spoke to him. I wasn't sure if he'd answer, but at least he'd know I was okay.

"Hey, Toby," I began. "You don't have to talk to me, but I thought you'd like to know that I am okay. I'll be back in a few months."

"Please, Vidie," he whispered so quietly I almost didn't hear it.

"I'll come back soon, I promise," I said, fighting back tears. "And I'll bring you something when I do. Will that be okay?"

"He nodded," Violet spoke for him. "I'm sure he'd like that."

"Good," I smiled. "I'll be back home before you know it."

"I think he's done," Violet said, a bit of sadness to her tone. "If he wants, would you be up to having another phone call?"

"Absolutely," I said. "You can call anytime, and I'll answer. Promise."

Not sure if the phone call changed anything, or helped Toby in any way, but it was worth a shot. Violet and I talked a little more before hanging up. I hoped that Toby would call me. I worried about him more than I thought I should.

The boy had stolen my heart as much as the rest of the family had already. Would he be okay with Joshua? Would he open up to me when I got back? Or would Toby want nothing to do with me when he found out?

"You okay?" Zachariah asked, leaning against the doorway.

"Yeah," I answered. "Just worried."

"About what?" he asked.

"Toby," I sighed. "What if he doesn't like my reasons for being gone? What if he wants nothing to do with me?"

"I don't think Toby would be anything but happy to see you," Zachariah answered, pulling me into a hug. I melted against his chest. "He has liked you since he first time he saw you. It's like the rest of the family, Avidya. No one could ever hate you, no matter how hard they tried to. You are light to the darkness in all of us."

"You make it sound so easy," I said, propping my chin on his chest. "You make it all seem so much easier than it really is. It's not all sunshine and roses."

"It's you that makes it easy," he said. "It's all you. No one else. You are the one that is easy."

"Did you just call me easy?" I asked with a glare.

"Well, I did get you with little effort," he winked before his mouth crashed to mine.

Instantly, I melted against his lips and body. I let him take control of the kiss, making sure not hurt me or take things any farther.

With his lips alone, he showed me just how easy it was to forgive and forget. He showed me how much he loved me and would do anything for me.

As my stomach filled with butterflies, I knew he was it for me. There would be no more running or second guessing our motives in life. There was no more fighting against each other's choices.

We were one, and would always be one. Nothing would be able to stand between us again.

Pulling back, his eyes were bright with happiness and love.

"Shall we go do something before I take you on that bed?" he asked.

"I'd love to do that, but yes please," I blushed.

Yeah, now was not the time to let him have his wicked way with me. I couldn't wait to get the all clear from the doctor next week. Now was not the time to test the links of fate with expanding our family. I don't think either one of us could handle that.

## Chapter 31

### *Zachariah*

I never expected to fall into step being a father. I never wanted children, which everyone around me knew without a doubt. Kids and I just never got along. Ever. I didn't try to be different to cater to children of any age. I never catered to *anyone*. That was until I found Avidya.

With Avidya, everything changed. She made me see how things were more than just black and white. Avidya brought things to light. She made me want to live; made me be something *more* than just a man that tried to control my men to bring in money.

That life was nothing when comparing it to the three of us now. Losing my brothel, losing my club, losing what I had worked so hard to get and my status in the world was no longer that important when put next to my wife and child.

Now as I held Joshua in my arms, watching Avidya sleep beside me on the couch, I knew I would never be able to give these two up. I questioned myself on why I didn't want Avidya to have a kid. I asked myself why I didn't want one. And why didn't I give it more thought before jumping to conclusions?

Thinking over everything, I was scared that any child we had would be used against me. Everyone around me could be used against me. I didn't want some nameless child to be forced into the life I led. I didn't want its choices taken away from it.

My choices were all my own as I grew up. I didn't have to be in the mafia. I didn't have to take such a part in it. I did, though. I wasn't as big of a rule abiding man as my father and grandfather, but I still took part in many things.

Holding my son, I knew that things wouldn't have to be the same. He would have as much of a choice as I had when it came to being in the family of more than just a member. He would be protected, just like Avidya and anyone else. We protect our own before anything else. I knew we all would be fine in the end.

Joshua would be able to grow up having anything he desired. He'd have the same choices as I did as a child, and there was no guarantee that he'd pick the same paths that I did. I wouldn't keep him hidden from the world. I wouldn't keep secrets. I'd let him know what I did and let him choose when he was of age.

I just hoped that Avidya would be okay with that.

I knew we all would be okay. I'd do everything in my power to make sure that we were.

Why? Because I was Zachariah Melendez.

I was pleasantly surprised that Avidya let me kiss her, though. I had missed it so much, I never wanted to stop. Her lips called to me as much as the rest of her.

She was soft and warm, and I wanted to do so much more than just kissing her. I knew we couldn't rush things, not yet. But fuck, I wanted her more than anything.

It really was amazing how she made everything better. She didn't hold anything against me from the past. Avidya was open to put the past behind us and move on.

Looking back at Josh as he stared up at me from my arms, my heart swelled in love for this little one. Green eyes blinked at me, like he knew just who I was. His little hand was wrapped around my pinky as I held the bottle so he could eat. He even made these adorable little sounds as he drank his milk.

How could I not ever want a child after holding this one in my arms?

I wished more than anything that I could have been here for his mother, for him, while he was in the hospital. I wished that someone would have told me about all this—all that I was missing out on.

What did Avidya look like while pregnant? What were her cravings? Was she emotional? Did she cry herself to sleep, wanting me here just as much as I wanted to be here?

Would she want another child later on?

God, I wasn't sure I'd be up for that. But if it happened, I would let it. I would never go against Avidya's beliefs again. I was an idiot to do so the first time.

"He's up already?" Avidya yawned, pushing herself up so she sat.

"He thinks so," I said. "Not that anyone would agree with midnight playtime."

"This is his new time to be wide away," she laughed, her eyes brighter than they had when I showed up on her doorstep.

"How did you do all this on your own?" I asked. Given, it was only a week, but still it had to be hard.

"Luckily, I don't have to go to work, so I slept during the day a bit," she shrugged. "They say it gets easier, but yeah, I don't think so."

"No, it only gets harder," I agreed. "I'm sure once we get back, everyone will offer to watch him every night."

"Oh, that I don't doubt," she said, leaning her head against my shoulder. She put one hand on Joshua's toes as they tended to stick out. He hated having his toes covered, I found out. "I'm sure they'd all be happy to keep him all the time."

"Most likely," I muttered. Louder, "They all want pictures."

"I haven't taken any," she shrugged. "Krissy has."

"Why not?" I asked.

"I don't have a phone that will do them," she said like I should have known. "And I haven't gotten around to getting a camera or a phone to do so. But when I do, Krissy will send all of them to me."

"How have you lived without all that?" I asked. No phone, no internet, and hardly anything she owned was here.

"I don't need any of it," she answered. "I've lived without it before, so now was no different."

I didn't know what to say to that, so I didn't say anything at all.

"Where did you work?"

"I worked in a home daycare part time. It kept me busy enough to keep my mind from going in circles," she answered. "I won't be returning, but I think they all expected that once you showed up."

"You can if you want," I said.

"There's no point for a few weeks," she shrugged. "I don't really want to go back now, anyhow."

"You sure?" I wouldn't care if she wanted to. I'd be happy to take care of Joshua if she wanted to go back to work.

"I'm sure," she said, her voice strong. "There's not much point in working with little sleep, and for only a few weeks."

"We don't have to go back at all, you know," I mused.

"Yes, we do," she said, looking up at me. "Everyone wants to meet the new addition, and I promised Toby I would go back. I always planned eventually go back anyhow. I only have two friends here, and we'll keep in touch through Facebook and phone calls. Plus, it's not that long of a drive to meet up every couple of months."

"You have it all figured out, don't you?" I asked, surprised.

"Yeah," she said sheepishly. "I've had a lot of thinking time."

"Guess that makes it easier," I mused.

"I've always known I'd end up going back," she shrugged. "I just wasn't sure when that would be."

"Would it have been sooner if I showed up before I

did?" I couldn't help but ask.

"Most likely, yes," she answered without having to think about it. "I figured you'd show up one day."

"And I did," I stated.

"You did. And I'm ready to go back once we get the all clear from the doctor on Josh," she went on.

Although he was born a preemie, other than his size, he didn't really act like one. Yes, he wanted food often, but I was sure that was a normal newborn thing. If I hadn't known he was born so early, I wouldn't have been able to tell.

Avidya had the all clear from her own doctor just a few days ago, but we still planned to take things slow. Mostly so that her birth control would be in full effect before we just jumped back into bed. I knew we had to take everything one step at a time.

It would be well worth it in the end.

## Chapter 32

## Avidya

"Do you have everything?" Krissy asked as she looked over the many boxes that were packed into the small U-Haul that was now attached to the dark red SUV that Zachariah was determined to buy. I really didn't have that much to take with us. Only a few boxes were filled with Joshua's clothing and blankets. His swing was folded up between everything, along with the bassinet that Krissy demanded that I take with me.

The portable crib like bassinet that Taylor had gotten me was also packed in there somewhere, too.

"I think it's all too much," I laughed. "But yes."

"Call me when you get in," she demanded.

"Of course," I replied. "We'll be just fine. May take us twice as long to get there, but we will."

"Do you have to leave?" Catrina asked, again for the twentieth time.

"I do," I said, bending down to her level. "My family misses me and would like to meet Josh now that he can travel."

"But can't you come back?" she asked.

"You'll get to see me again in a few months," I promised. "I'll call you as often as I can."

"I don't want you to go," she cried, flinging her arms around my neck.

"Neither do I," Krissy said, running a hand over the top of the girl's red hair. "But her family misses her. She'll be back. If not, we will go to her to see her."

"Promise?" Catrina asked.

"Pinky promise," Krissy smiled.

"Okay," she sighed, seeming to be okay with that as she pulled away from me. "Mommy?"

"Yes?" Krissy asked.

"Can I have a baby brother now?" she asked, her head cocked to the side.

"No," Krissy said, hiding her laugh. "Maybe when we find a daddy first."

"He can be our daddy," Catrina said, pointing to my husband.

"Sorry, Miss," Zachariah said, winking her way. "I'm only a daddy to one little boy."

"Oh," Catrina said, feeling dejected. "Guess I'll have to find one then."

"Good luck with that," Zachariah laughed. "Are you all set?"

"Yep," I answered.

"Good. Josh has been fed and changed, and strapped into his seat," Zachariah said. "Just have to lock up the house."

"Will it stay empty?" Krissy asked.

"Probably for a week or so," Zachariah answered. "But you can expect someone else to move in sometime in the future. My family aren't total monsters. We do help people in need."

"It better be someone more social than Taylor," Krissy laughed.

"No guarantees," Zachariah laughed. "But I can keep that in mind."

"I really like him," Krissy staged whispered to me, causing me to laugh. "You have to keep him around."

"He is pretty likable on most days," I agreed.

After bidding us goodbye, and getting more than enough hugs to last until the next time Catrina would be able to see me, we headed out and back towards home.

Home.

The one place I knew I would go back to. I wasn't sure if it would be now or years later, but I would have gone back one day.

On the way back, we had to stop every couple of

hours to feed Joshua. What would have been an eight-hour trip ended up being a near twelve-hour trip. It helped that Zachariah didn't take any round about ways back home. It was a pretty straight shot from point A to point B.

The entire way back, Zachariah and I talked about what we wanted to do with everything that went around in our lives. It was almost like we hadn't been apart for almost a year.

"Have you been writing in the journals?" he asked. He had seen my stack of journals, some filled and some still empty while I was packing this past week.

"Yes," I answered. "You didn't get any of them from your father?"

"No," he said.

"Oh. I sent a few to him and he was supposed to give them to you. No wonder you were so surprised when you showed up," I said. Although I never wrote in them with what I was pregnant, I did hint at it more than once. I had just sent out my third shipment of journals a couple days before my husband had showed up at my doorstep.

"That would explain the box I hadn't opened," he mused. "My father dropped a box off at the house and I thought it had to do with work. Just told me to look through them."

"And you didn't," I guessed. I wasn't all that surprised, as Carlos was even sure what was in the box, only knew it had come from me.

"If I had known they were from you, I would have jumped right in," he said, glancing at me. "But I thought they had to do with work."

"That's okay," I shrugged. "You don't really need to read them now."

"You can count on me reading every single word you wrote," he said, his voice firm. "Everything you have to say, written or spoken, is important to me."

"Just know that I wasn't in the best place when I wrote the stuff in there," I said.

"I don't care," he said. "I'll still read it. I wasn't in the best place either, so we're even."

"Do you still want in the lifestyle?" he asked after a few moments as we kept on driving.

"The BDSM?" I clarified.

"Yes," he answered.

"Yeah, I think so," I said after thinking it over. I needed it. It made me feel like I had control over something in my life. What I had experienced before I left was exciting and something I quickly learned I wanted.

"Good," he said as though he was afraid that I

didn't want that. "We'll have to go slow, just like before. But I think everything that was laid out can stay the same, if you agree."

"I think so," I said. "We will just go at whatever we both feel."

Why was there a need to have things laid out for us? We both knew what we wanted and needed. Just having each other was more than enough. The rest could be figured out later.

By the time we got home, it was well after dark and we were both tired. Unloading everything would wait until the morning. Although it wouldn't have mattered much since Joshua wasn't a huge sleeper and didn't seem to be becoming one any time soon.

Zachariah beat me to getting Joshua out of the back seat as I got out of the front. He really was surprising me at every corner, and I wasn't going to complain.

It all made me love him more.

It also made me feel slightly sad that I didn't let him experience everything next to my side as I went through my pregnancy. I hoped I did the right thing, though.

"This will probably be the only time we have to ourselves here for a while," Zach said, taking my hand as he led me to the front of the house.

"Did anyone know we were coming back today?" I asked. Technically, it was night already, but did it really matter?

"Nope," he said, unlocking and unalarming the door so we could enter. "I wanted us to have at least one night. I'm sure they will know come morning, but for tonight we will not be bothered."

"You sure about that?" I joked. His phone liked to ring constantly day and night it seemed. Not that he answered it every time.

"No," he laughed. "But *I* want one night with just the three of us. Everyone else can wait until tomorrow."

Once in the house, Zachariah left me to unbuckle Joshua as he went to make a bottle. The diaper bag sat beside the carrier on the couch. I knew come morning, everyone would show up and we wouldn't have a moment to ourselves. But otherwise, it really was good to be home. I missed this. All of this.

I smiled at Zachariah as he handed over the bottle to me.

"I'm going to go change, then I'll be back. After you feed him, there's something I want to show you," he said before kissing the top of my head.

I nodded, letting my eyes close at the contact.

How could he always make me feel so loved with a simple touch?

# Chapter 33

## Zachariah

I took a quick shower and slipped on cotton pants before returning back to my wife and child. I had other motives for coming up before Avidya, which she would quickly find out.

I didn't lie to her. None of my family knew we came back yet, as they thought we would be getting a hotel a few hours away to stay in before making our way home. I wanted one night without being bothered by them. I wanted just one night with my wife and son before things got all crazy again.

On the way home, I told her what had happened to the club. She was surprised, but not too much at who had sat the fire. One stupid fucker that was upset I wasn't setting up a new brothel in the city limits. I didn't need that to get money. Instead, I set up a women's shelter downtown that would help the women that wanted a better life.

The new club would be a bit closer to home and in a nicer part of town. The same rules would apply, but there would be a few changes here and there. I planned to have it up and running in six months or so as long as everything went according to plan. A few more rooms had been added for both subs and Doms to take part in whatever they fancied, almost anything, anyhow. I would never allow some things that men thought were appropriate.

Once I was done changing, I found Avidya in the living room as she finished feeding our son. I was happy she didn't decide to breastfeed, because I wanted to help as much as I possibly could. Avidya had said that the NICU stay made it too hard for her milk supply to work, so the bottle was what ended up working.

I knew that once everyone knew we were back home, someone would constantly be here for one thing or another to see the new baby. I'd also have to get back to work and oversee a few things that I had left unfinished when I went after my wife.

"Where do you plan to have him sleep tonight?" she asked when she saw me.

"Come with me and I'll show you," I said, holding my hand out to her.

She took my hand as she put Joshua to her chest. I led her upstairs and stopped at the doorway of the room that had once had been intended for her.

She gasped as I turned on the light.

Inside, the queen-sized bed had been removed and stored away to make room for a crib and dresser, along with a shelf for stuffed animals and a few books that had already been bought. The dark oak crib was low to the ground. The ends were rounded at the top like a sleigh bed.

In front of the crib was a light cream soft rug that matched the soft green painted walls. A rocking chair sat in front of the closet, waiting to be used.

"Wow," Avidya sighed, wide eyed.

"When Violet and Mom heard that you would be coming back, they wanted to set up this room for you. You never hinted about really setting anything up, so they asked if it was okay to do so. I thought it would be nice to not have to worry about setting any of this up," he explained as though I'd be upset about it already being done for me.

"It's amazing," she sighed, entering all the way in. "I don't know what to say."

"There's more, but it's in our room," I said, stuffing my hands in the pockets of my sleep pants.

"What more could there possibly be?" she asked.

"I'll show you," I said, nodding towards our room.

With wide eyes, she passed me and went into our room, stopping once more as she spotted my own little surprise that I left her.

"How?" she asked.

Beside our bed, on her side, stood a bassinet that looked to be antique. White frilly bedding surrounded the inside. The entire thing was made out of metal, but looked like it was created to be up to date.

"I had it handmade," I said, almost afraid she wouldn't like it. "That's what I was on the phone about so much that one day. Sturdy enough to hold him up to a year, although he'd probably fall out when he can stand. The bedding was also handmade, and there's another set in the closet for it."

"I love it," she said in awe. "It's perfect. Thank you, Zach."

"You're welcome," I said, happy that she did like it. "It also rocks."

"Thank you," she said, tears filling her eyes. A moment later, she gave me a light, but tight one-armed hug as Josh was still in her arms.

"I'd do anything for you," I said, wrapping my arms around both of them. "I want you to be happy."

"I will be," she said against my chest. "You make me happy."

"I'll keep trying to make sure it stays that way," I said.

She had to see that my happiness would be with her being happy. I would never stop making her happy. I would show her more with this second chance that I got.

She pulled back, teary eyed still, and turned around. After placing Joshua down in the bassinet, she took a seat on the edge of the bed. "How long do you think they will hold off in the morning?"

"Not long," I grimaced. "I'll try to hold them off as long as possible though."

"Just make me breakfast," she joked.

"That I can do," I smiled. "Get ready for bed. I'll take first waking."

"You sure?" she asked after yawning.

"Positive," I replied. There were still a few things I needed to do before I could go to sleep for the night. I knew that they could certainly wait, but I wanted to get it done while I had the chance and before tomorrow got busy once more.

"Okay," she said. "Thank you again."

"Of course, Vidie," I said with a smile. "I love you more than you can ever imagine."

"I love you to," she said sincerely.

## Chapter 34

### Avidya

I had no idea what time Zachariah finally came to bed, but what I did know was that I didn't wake up once after I fell asleep. I woke up in a panic, thinking something had happened to Josh. I found his bed empty, so I gathered that Zach had taken care of him all night long. At least that was what I was hoping. I didn't think Zachariah would do anything.

Although I didn't want to get up, I knew I needed to. I desperately needed a shower and to get dressed before anyone showed up to the house. The bed was far too comfortable to move from, and I ended up dozing back off for a while after laying my head back on my pillow.

I couldn't remember the last time I had slept through the night. It had to have been over a year now. It really was amazing how things changed over time.

I finally woke up when Zachariah came to shake me awake after I had dozed back off, telling me that his parents were here and would like to see me.

"What time is it?" I asked, rubbing the sleep from my eyes as I turned onto my back.

"Almost eleven," he said softly. "I let you sleep for a while."

"I didn't mean to sleep so late," I stretched my body out. This bed was like a vacuum, pulling me into its depths.

"You needed it," he said, moving some of my hair off of my face. The pads of his fingers barely made contact with my skin. "Just figured you'd like to be dressed and awake before Toby got here. Apparently, he's a bit excited to see you."

"I think someone else is too," I said, letting my eyes trail down his body.

"Well *he* can wait," he grunted out. "I'll leave you to shower and dress."

I could hear the unsaid words about him being happy to join me if I needed help. Now really wasn't the time. Although it did seem like an appealing idea.

"I'll be down soon," I said, pushing myself up.

It didn't take me long to shower and throw on some clothes on that were here from before I left. I braided my hair off to the side so it wasn't in my face all day long. My hair was now down to my waist and I refused to cut it. I liked my long hair even though I had no idea what to do with it half the time.

Walking down the stairs, I heard the voices of Julia

and Carlos. Rounding the corner, I couldn't help but smile as both of them gushed over my son.

When Zachariah spotted me, he instantly came to my side and pulled me against him. "I think we lost our son."

"I could just love on him all day long," Julia said, giving me a smile. "You look well."

"A good night sleep helped," I shrugged.

"Zach explained a bit of it to us," Julia said. "I could have stayed longer if you weren't up to me leaving yet. I wouldn't have minded."

"You have helped," I said, giving them a smile. "And it was more than enough. I needed to do things on my own, and I did. I still would have been able to handle it."

"Well, know that we won't be letting you get away with us not helping now," Julia said.

Not even five minutes later, it seemed like everyone else showed up. The house was instantly filled with laughter, love, and family.

I didn't know I had missed this all so much. I never thought that I needed a family until I no longer had it.

The last ones to arrive were Violet and Toby, who seemed to have had a meltdown shortly before coming here.

Excusing myself from Zach's side as he talked to Travis, I made my way to Toby, who would hardly look at me as he hid behind Violet. His face was red, his eyes even redder as though he had cried not all that long ago.

"Sorry," she whispered low enough we were the only ones that could hear. "He's a bit upset today. Long night of not much sleep. Most nights are a touch and go as it is."

"You don't have to explain to me," I said. "He's able to have a bad day. He's been through a lot more than any of us here have."

"Yes, he has," Violet agreed, pulling me into a hug. In my ear she whispered, "He doesn't know about the baby yet. He was so excited to see you last night he couldn't sleep. And then this morning he didn't want to take a shower before coming over here. I don't know how he'll react to the baby today after everything. His emotions are getting the better of him today."

I could hear the concern in her voice. She had no idea how Toby would react to the baby, and neither did I.

"Don't worry about it," I said, returning the hug. "I'll make sure he understands the situation."

Pulling back, she gave me a smile before laying a hand on Toby's shoulder.

"Hey there," I smiled at him. He had grown quite a bit over the months, and was now almost to my shoulders. His dark hair was cut and still slightly damp. "How are you doing today?"

He shrugged in answer, fiddling with the hem of his shirt.

"Having a bad day?" I asked.

"Most days are," Melio said, pulling me into yet another side hug. "But we're getting there. Just glad to have you back."

"I'm happy to be back," I said with a smile. I let my body lean into Melio's, not that he gave me much choice as he held me tightly. "I've missed you all."

"Well, you wouldn't have had to miss us if you'd just have stayed here," Melio declared.

"Yeah, yeah," I said, rolling my eyes. "I had to go find myself."

"That you certainly did," Melio said before letting me go.

"Do you want to go outside with me, Toby?" I asked him, letting my eyes stay on him even though he didn't look my way.

He shrugged both shoulders.

"How about this," I hedged. "I'm going outside to

take a small walk to get a break from all these people. If you would like to join, you can."

"What about Joshua?" Melio asked.

"Zach will watch over him," I said with a smile. "He's getting pretty good at that."

"Huh," Melio said in thought. "Never thought I'd see that."

"He's doing pretty well, surprisingly," I replied.

With one last look at Toby, I made my way out the front door. Everyone here really only wanted to see Joshua, so I knew that I wouldn't be missed. Zachariah would be the first that noticed I wasn't in the house, but I figured someone would let him know where I went if he didn't come looking for me first.

I had a feeling that Toby wasn't a huge fan of all the people either, least of all with people he wasn't too thrilled about as it was.

I took my time to go down each step once I was outside. I had no idea if Toby would follow me, but I felt it should be in his hands to take the step if he wanted to talk to me. I knew he wasn't happy with me, but if Zach could forgive me for running, then I was sure that Toby would be able to in time.

The sun was out and already warming up the air as

the minutes passed. It was slightly chilly, but not too bad. The grass was starting to turn a nice green color, and I spotted a few guards that were hanging around.

Of course, Zachariah still had guards around. He was a man of power, and anyone wouldn't have thought twice about taking any one of us out. Just because Aaron was taken care of didn't mean that there were no other threats out there.

I was about ten feet from the house when I heard rushed, but quiet, footsteps coming up behind me. I didn't turn around or stop as I already was walking at a pretty slow pace. I had guessed that Toby would have taken longer to follow me, if he did at all.

Once he was right beside me, head down, I started to talk to him. It was what had worked before, so I hoped it would do the trick again.

"I really am sorry I left. I had to keep someone safe, and by leaving I could do that. There was no other way to protect someone that I loved very much." I paused, thinking of how to say what needed to be said. Was there a way to say everything that needed to be said? I wasn't so sure.

"I won't be leaving again now that I know everyone I care about is safe," I went on.

"Why did he want to hurt you?" he asked so quietly I almost didn't catch it.

"Who?" I asked, not sure what person he meant. There were a number of people that wanted to hurt me. Some were deader than a doornail, and other would find out that if they did mess with me, they would wish for death.

"Your...Zachariah?" he asked, still not looking at me.

"He didn't want to hurt me. It wasn't actions, but words that really hurt, though. Zach didn't want me to have something, and said some hurtful things," I explained. "I didn't agree with the way he said such things, and I had to leave to keep something I wanted very much."

"And that's what made you leave, right?" he asked.

"Mostly, yes," I answered. "He didn't want me to have any kids. He said he'd never allow me to have one."

"Then why come back?" he asked tearfully.

"Because he came and found me. He apologized to me," I answered. "I didn't come back just for him. I came back for everyone. Including you. I missed everyone."

"Violet said you had a kid," he said, kicking a small rock out of his way.

"I did," I said, not hiding that fact. "And he's here,

too."

"Won't Zach take him away?" he asked. "That's what happened to me. My dad didn't want me and took me away from my mom after killing her."

"No, Zach won't ever take him away," I said. "If he tried, I'd kill him first."

Toby froze at my words.

"I wouldn't really, but I'd want to," I was quick to say. "He's not a kid person, but he's trying now. And that's what counts. Some people can change."

"Not all," Toby whispered.

"No, not all do," I agreed.

"Have you changed?" he asked, looking up at me for a moment.

"I don't think so," I said, shaking my head. "I'm still just me. I may be a mom now, but I still like and do the same stuff as before."

"Then why couldn't you have taken me with you if you didn't change?" he asked.

"Toby, sweetheart," I sighed, pulling him to me. He went against me willingly, wrapping his arms around my waist. "You couldn't have gone with me. Violet and Melio would have been devastated. Besides I wasn't happy, and you wouldn't have been either. I was sad and had to figure stuff out before I came back. I had to make sure that my baby would be welcomed by Zach and everyone before I ever thought of returning."

"Don't leave again, please," he cried against my chest.

"I promise I won't," I said, laying my head on his, fighting back my own tears. "I can't or it'd break me. Again."

We stood there for a few minutes in silence, hanging on to one another. The only sounds that were heard were the birds chirping in the trees around us.

"Would you like to see my baby?" I asked as we both pulled apart.

"Sure," he shrugged, trying to act as if he didn't care. I could tell he wanted to see my baby, and I think I would never get to hold my son again afterwards.

I had a feeling that Toby and Josh would quite possibly be inseparable soon enough. As much as Catrina would be when they came to visit.

# Chapter 35

## Avidya

I was right in my assumptions. Once Toby laid eyes on my Joshua, he was a totally different person. He wanted to know how to do everything for the baby. I think Toby was more protective over my little boy than even Zachariah was, and that was hard to pass.

"I think we found our babysitter for the rest of our lives," Zachariah joked as he stood behind me with his arms wrapped loosely across my torso.

"I bet they will fight over who watches him constantly," I said. Not that I minded. I really didn't want to be bombarded by everyone every day, though. I needed my time with my son as much as I needed time with my husband.

"When can he do a sleepover?" Toby asked as his eyes bounced between me and Violet, who now was holding the baby.

"Not few a few months," I answered. I didn't want my baby anywhere without me for too long. He was so little. Letting Zachariah take care of Joshua during the night was a stretch alone, but that was only happening because I had to have sleep.

"Maybe you could stay over one night and help me take care of him?" Zachariah hinted.

"Maybe," Toby said wide eyed. The surprise on his face was apparent. It wasn't often at all that Zachariah willingly talked to anyone younger than him.

"Wow, you really have changed," Melio joked.

"Did no such thing," Zachariah stated.

I shook my head at their antics. My husband did change for the better. We may have had our differences a year ago, but now things were so much better. The time apart did do us both good as we got time to figure out that some things were just not as important as we had first thought.

~oOo~

Before I knew it, everything was coming together all too well. For some reason, I kept thinking something would happen to cause me to doubt coming back. Zachariah did much better at the whole father thing than I ever thought he would. His entire family was surprised, too.

Lynn tried to contact me once, and after listening to her side of the story, I couldn't really find it in myself to care why she did what she did. She was the woman that raised me, but never stood up against Cody on how I was raised. She may have been in an abusive relationship and didn't know how to get out, but that didn't mean I could forgive her.

She lied to me. She deceived me.

Yes, Lynn may have gotten me into Zachariah's hands and that alone made my life so much better than it could certainly have ended up being. But I couldn't forgive her. She was also responsible for my best friend's death.

I didn't want her to meet my son and I didn't want her anywhere around either of us. I knew it was harsh, but I didn't trust her after what she let Cody do, and what she kept hidden from me my entire life.

I couldn't trust Lynn anywhere around my child.

Surprisingly, she understood. She said she hoped that I would someday change my mind, but she wouldn't push. I was welcome to call her anytime.

Coming back to this life, I had expected things to be different between me and everyone. I wasn't sure why, but I just had this feeling things would have been strained. Nothing was, though. I fell right back into where I had left them all.

I had been back for three months, and luckily

Zachariah had put his foot down about not having everyone bombard us constantly, unless one of us asked for help. He knew that I wanted to take care of Josh without a bunch of people around at every moment.

Once a month, until now, someone had stayed the night to watch Joshua so Zach and I could get a full night of sleep. Joshua still wasn't a huge sleeper, so that one night was more than welcome. He never left the house without me. Not until tonight anyhow.

Tonight, Zachariah wanted us to do another double date with Travis and Kenna, since the last one failed so miserably. This time instead of at the club, it was at an upscale restaurant where the four of us would be mostly secluded.

Per Zachariah's request, I dressed in a little black dress that dipped in the back. The material flowed easily over my body, hugging my curves only slightly. My blond hair was left in soft waves down my back.

He wore black slacks and a dark blue button up shirt, and my heart soared at seeing him all dressed up for me. He knew how much I loved it when he didn't shave, leaving a dusting of hair on his face. Every time I looked at this man, my heart beat twice in speed and I was filled with so much desire, I wanted to let him have his wicked way with me.

Soon. Soon he would do just that.

I also wore the necklace that he had given me that was meant to show the world that I was his. I couldn't deny that it was one of my most favorite necklaces ever. The cross hung down past my collar bone. An infinity symbol held the chain around my neck.

Although it was dainty, it fit me perfectly.

Zachariah wanted to get me something that would be able to hold up to being pulled on, and I knew he would soon since Josh was a pro at wrapping his little fingers around everything he could. I think that Zach was happier about the fact that I put his ring back on my finger.

After leaving the car to be parked by the Valet, I hooked my arm through Zachariah's at the elbow. The place was lit up with lights and it was so tall, I couldn't see the top of the building form the sidewalk. This restaurant screamed money.

Along the sidewalk was a line of people waiting to be let in, who were all dressed as nicely as we were. Zach bypassed them, walking right up to the front where a man in a work uniform stood with a clipboard.

"Reservation for four," Zachariah said.

"Go right on in, Mr. Melendez," the bouncer said,

opening the door open for us to enter.

"Let me guess, you own this place?" I asked.

"I own many places, my sweet," he said, winking down at me.

My husband was one of many powerful men in this town, so I shouldn't have been all that surprised that he owned this place among others.

"I just haven't shown you off enough for everyone here to know who you are to me. Given time, everyone will know exactly who you are and you will get the same treatment wherever you wish to go in this town," he said as a waiter led us to the back of the place.

That was not what I wanted, and I gave him a look. He simply shrugged at me, not at all concerned about that.

"I want to show you off, and to do that, people who will know who you are," he stated.

Inside, the carpet was a dark red color that blended in nicely with the oak tables that were covered with white cloths and matching chairs.

Although the inside was as antique looking as the outside, it was extravagant. There were a number of people sitting about eating their meals as we made our way to the table.

Once at the table, Zachariah held the chair out for

me before taking his own seat beside me.

"Is there anything I can get you?" the waiter asked.

"Just four glasses of water to start, please," Zachariah said.

"Perfect," the waiter replied before walking off.

"Do I want to know how many other places you own?" I asked, trying to appear as if I fit in here. I felt out of place.

"Probably not," Zachariah laughed. "This one is not as fancy as some of the other places. But I thought this would be one of the few places you'd enjoy food wise."

"You know you don't have to impress me," I told him as he took his own seat.

"Oh, I know," he said, a smile spreading across his lips. "But I want to. I want to show the world that you are mine. They have to know that my heart is taken by the most beautiful woman alive."

At his words, my cheeks flooded in color, causing him to laugh before leaning in and kissing my cheek lightly.

"I missed that blush," he whispered.

Before I could reply, Travis and Kenna both arrived, taking their seats. It still amazed me how their relationship was conducted and how they worked so well together. Kenna was a Mistress and Travis was her sub. I never would have imagined him to be that way, and it was still a little strange to see it now.

"Hello, Avidya," Kenna said my way after taking her seat. "How are you today?"

"Doing pretty well," I answered. I wasn't nearly as nervous as I was the first time we had a double date, thank goodness.

"Good," she smiled. "You two getting along these days?"

"Why wouldn't we?" Zachariah asked.

"Just wondering," she shrugged.

"How are you two doing?" I asked.

"Really good," Kenna answered. "Travis here got in trouble for talking today when I told him not to, so please excuse his lack of doing so now."

"I don't want to know," I muttered with a blush. Travis simply smiled my way, causing my cheeks to heat once more.

"You probably don't," Kenna laughed. "When do you two plan to take more into the bedroom?"

"Soon," Zachariah answered. "It's been way too long, and we've been a bit busy."

"I don't want Josh hearing, nor do we want to be

interrupted," I shrugged.

The topic had come up a few times the past few weeks. We were both ready for more, but having a child in the house, or someone watching him in the house, kind of put us both off. Yes, his family knew what kind of sex life we both liked but that didn't change that fact that we were uncomfortable doing it.

We had sex a number of times, but nothing like what we both craved. I wanted more. I wanted to be pushed to my limits and not worry about how much noise was made.

"I bet I know what you two will be doing tonight," Travis said, wagging his eyebrows. A moment later, he stiffened as Kenna did something to him under the table.

"Do you plan to torture the man?" Zachariah laughed.

"He loves it," Kenna returned, shooting a sexy smile towards my brother. "He knows what will happen every time he talks tonight. It was his idea so he could at least talk to his sister."

At my widened eyes, she was quick to explain. "I'm not hurting him. I know his limits. If he wants me to stop, he'll tell me."

"I'm okay, sis," Travis said my way. "You'll love

certain things when you get more comfortable with Zach."

"If you say so," I said, not so sure of that myself. I don't think I could ever let Zach tease me while in public like this. At home, he had a few times and I loved it.

"Public display doesn't seem like her thing," Zach said, not upset. "But that's okay. I'm not big on them much myself, as you know."

We really were meant for each other.

Every time Travis talked, or close to it, Kenna would do something under the table, causing him to squirm and fidget in his seat. One time, he nearly even choked on his food.

I couldn't help but burst out laughing.

God, I had missed all this.

For the rest of dinner, talk went well. Travis and Kenna talked about the new club that would be opening up in less than a month, and how they were going to set things up. Zachariah did mention that he wanted me to see it before the doors open, to give him my view of how I saw it because he wanted to do something a little bit different this time around.

I agreed, only because I wanted to know everything there was to know about the man that I loved. Things between us were completely different now.

## Chapter 36

### Avidya

I was full of excitement at what was to come. I needed him like I needed air to breathe. Since living with Zachariah, and the first time he took me in his bed, I couldn't get enough of him. I would never have enough of him. I loved sex with him and only him.

He was the only man that could cause my heart to flutter with one simple look. My husband was the only man that ever knew me so personally.

Laying on my front, I pushed my ass into the air, drawing his attention to the task at hand as he slowly ran his hand down my back, across my ass cheeks, and to the junction between my thighs. I had my head lying on my folded hands on the bed, as instructed. I moaned, when he stuck a finger into me, and I clamped down around him.

"Stay," he said as he left me where I was, naked on the bed and dripping with arousal before moving to the dresser where a few toys were laid out.

He came back a few seconds later and after setting the things down next to me, he began to massage my back, loosening any knots that might be there. There weren't that many but it was relaxing anyway, I closed my eyes, loving the feel of him making me feel so relaxed. He has always taken care of me since I came to live with him.

"Are you sure about this, Avidya?" Zachariah asked as he reached the top of my butt cheeks, right were my hips met, massaging me and making me moan.

"Absolutely," I whispered out. "I've waited too long for this."

"Okay," Zachariah said calmly. He always asked before trying something new to make sure I was all for whatever we had planned before going through with it. "Be right back, I'm gonna put some music on."

I kept my eyes closed as he plugged his iPhone into the speaker that was set up across the room.

"Just to make sure you understood, this is not a scene but you can use the safe words if you need at any time. The words are yellow if you need me to slow down and red if you need me to stop. I will go slow, but you have to tell me if I hurt you. It may be a bit uncomfortable after a while," Zachariah said as he helped flip my body over so I looked up at his him. His eyes were alight with need.

"Understood, sir," I moaned, not able to help but be in a submissive zone when it came to trying something new.

He was right when he said I was a perfect woman for him.

His mouth crashed to mine in a heated frenzy, and I didn't disappoint him in returning the kiss.

Before I could lace my fingers through his soft hair, he took ahold of both my wrists, pinning them above my head by one hand. His other hand trailed down my body slowly, leaving a fiery trail of desire in its wake.

"So eager," Zachariah said. I could feel my lower belly tighten and warm. I wanted him now more than ever.

"For you," I breathed out as his hand slowly made its way down to my wet core.

He slipped a single finger into me, causing me to grasp out a breath once more. I never could understand how he knew my body so well.

He brought me near orgasm before withdrawing his fingers leaving me a whimpering mess. He left the bed, leaving me alone for a moment.

I couldn't lie still, needing friction and wanting release.

"Turn over again," he stated, pulling away far enough so I could do as he commanded. "I want to spank that ass."

Zachariah made sure I was stable enough in my kneeling position, having enough strength to keep my ass in the air. My head hung down slightly as I waited for what he'd do next.

I didn't have to wait long before one *smack* landed on my ass cheek. I couldn't help but lean into the pain, wanting more.

It didn't hurt, but it was what I needed. I needed that slight shock to help my body destress.

"You okay?" Zachariah asked.

"Yes," I answered, pushing back against him, silently asking for more.

Faster, he gave me a few more swift swats before quickly lining himself up.

In one fluid motion, he slipped into me. We both moaned out as one as he stilled.

Slowly he slid in, little by little, letting me get accustomed to his size. Once he was all the way in, he stayed still, letting me get use to him being there. It burned at first as I adjusted to the size of his cock in me. It had been a while since we played. Too long.

Feeling ready, I gave the okay to Zachariah and he began to slowly, and lovingly, move out, then back in, slowly letting me get used to the fullness of him.

As one hand held my hip tightly, his other hand went to my clit.

"You are mine," he grunted out, his breath warm against my back.

"Yours," I panted, never fighting against that statement.

"I could get use to this," Zachariah panted out, increasing his pace. I panted along with him as he kneeled behind me, his front to my back with no space between us. "I'm not going to last much longer."

"So close," I managed to moan out, trying to push back at him, seeking something more to push me over the edge.

The hand on my hip left, going to my hair and pulling slightly. I lifted my head, following his lead as he took what he wanted from me. I would never let him do this if I hadn't wanted it, and that was even better.

Zachariah pinched my clit as he pushed harder into me, and I came. His cocked hit something deep inside me, and I saw bright stars in my vision. Zachariah pumped once, then twice more before stilling and emptying everything he had into the condom. Apparently, we were both in need of a quick release.

"We are so gonna have to do that again," Zachariah

panted out after pulling out of me. I collapsed onto the bed, spent and sedated with a smile on my face.

Zachariah left to go into the en-suite bathroom telling me to stay still until he got back. He returned after a few minutes with a warm wash cloth, cleaning me and soothing me as I lazily laid there, blinking at him.

He lifted me up taking me into the bathroom, setting me on the floor as he turned the water in the tub off. I hadn't even heart him turn it on to being with. He then helped me into the tub, telling me to scoot forward so he could join me. He took a clean washcloth and washed my body as I leaned against him. He asked me how I was feeling. And I replied I was feeling great. More than great.

I understood that he was worried about me, since it had been almost a year since we had sex, such roughly at that. Little did he know that I would never tire of him. Tire of this.

Even in his slight roughness, Zachariah would never be able to hurt me.

He was showing me how much he loved me with how he took care of me afterwards, knowing I was for once, worn out. It wasn't often he wore me out like this, and I loved it. The aftercare was almost better than the sex part, and any sub would agree to that.

Being cherished and loved with such care was something I didn't have growing up, so I basked in it every chance I got with my husband.

He helped me out of the tub, took a towel from the warming rack and dried every inch of my body lovingly. After he dried himself off, he lifted me again taking me back into the bedroom where he helped me back into bed.

"I love you, my wife," he whispered as he laid down beside me, brushing stray hairs from my face.

"I love you too, my husband," I mumbled sleepily through a yawn. I force myself to move, to lie mostly on top of him, my head on his shoulder, my leg flung over his and my hand on his chest. I was home.

# Chapter 37

## Zachariah

I never wanted to move. I loved the feeling of my wife lying on top of me, fast asleep. Her hair was splayed out around her, lying limply over the side of my arm. Her breaths were even, her chest rising with each one she took.

Last night had been more than I was expecting. So much more.

I loved my wife, but I loved it even more when she submitted to me. Somehow, she was able to lessen my need to taking control constantly in the bedroom.

Don't get me wrong, we still had moments where I wanted nothing more than flip her over my knee and spank her senseless. I knew she wasn't a child and I couldn't do that. Instead, I saved it for our bedroom activities. She'd have to get over the fear of Joshua hearing her, because I wasn't going to make us wait so long like that again. I made a mental note to make one of the spare rooms soundproof, because I was not going to hide my needs for the entire twenty years our son would no doubt live in this house.

My own needs wouldn't let me, and neither would

hers.

We really were meant for each other. I think God made her just for me.

"Morning," she mumbled. Her voice was rough with sleep.

"Morning, sweetheart," I replied. "Are you sore?"

"Hmmm," she hummed, still relaxed against me. "Not too bad, I think."

"Let me know if you are. It has been a while since we were so rough," I hedged, petting her hair. I loved that it was longer and fit in my hand easily like last night.

"Bossy," she giggled out, but not upset.

"Gotta take care of the love of my life," I shrugged.

We fell into an easy silence, enjoying each other. We both knew that this wouldn't last when Joshua came back home. The first night with him gone and I missed him.

"Should we get ready to go get our son?" I asked.

"You miss him too?" Avidya said, lifting her head to meet my eyes.

"More than I thought I would," I said, giving her a smile.

"I need to pee," Avidya said, pushing herself off of me and in turn, the bed. I groaned out, seeing her naked breasts. They were perfect, just like the rest of her.

"Quit staring," she muttered with a shake of her head on her way to the bathroom. Of course, she walked with purpose, showing off her round butt in the process.

"Then quit teasing me," I called after her.

She simply gave me a sexy smile over her shoulder.

That little tease.

I waited until the shower came on before I made my way to the bathroom, following her path. She was just getting in under the warm spray as I went to take a piss. I felt her eyes on my ass. A huge smile crossed my lips. She loved my ass as much as I loved hers.

After flushing and washing my hands, I stepped into the shower. Our clothes were left discarded around the room from our late-night activities.

Once I had my hands on her, I crashed my mouth to hers, taking control of her body as the water rushed over the both of us. She moaned into my mouth, pushing against my body as her body heated from the inside out.

"I'm going to take you here in this shower," I muttered as I trailed kisses down her neck.

"Please," she begged, grabbing ahold of my hair and pushing me against her body.

I took my time, trailing my mouth down to one peaked nipple. I took it into my mouth and sucked on it before slightly biting down around what I had in my mouth. At the slight pressure, not enough to cause her pain, Avidya gasped out loudly, dropping her head to her chest. Her hands pushed me harder against her breast, so I had to do it again.

"Zach," she moaned. I felt her pelvis push against me, trying to find friction she desperately wanted.

"Maybe I should make you wait," I said, pulling pack. I moved one hand to her other breast, tweaking the nipple.

"You wouldn't dare," she seethed, her voice breathy.

"Oh, I so would," I said, my voice dark with promise. "You'd go nuts all day, knowing what I did to you. You'd be wet all day thinking about what you *need* from me."

"I'd be wet all day either way," she spit at me, daring me.

Now, she was just egging me on. She wanted me to tease her.

And God, did I want to.

That would have to wait another day, because I was hard as a rock and didn't want to have a boner all day long around my family.

Instead, I gave her a look that spoke volumes. I could tease her all day long if I wanted it, because she would let me.

I put my mouth back on Avidya's, my hands going up to pin her arms above her head.

"Don't move them," I stated, slightly squeezing her wrists to prove what I was talking about.

At her nod, I reached over for a condom from the soap shelf and slipped it onto my hard cock. Then, placing both my hands to her hips, and pushed my cock into her warmth. She moaned at the feeling, spreading her legs slightly farther apart to give me a bit more room.

"One day soon, I'll make you scream so loud, the birds will fly away in fear," I grunted, pushing my cock into her over and over again.

I would have loved to tease her, but my own selfish needs wouldn't let me. I wanted to come as much as she did right this second.

This wasn't nice sweet lovemaking like the night before. Oh no. This was hard, rough, and everything in between.

"Mine," I growled before lightly biting her where her neck and shoulder met.

"Always," she agreed as her walls squeezed me

tightly as her orgasm consumed her.

I followed right along with her, spilling into her on a hard grunt myself.

I'd never tire of doing this. I'd never tire of my wife in any way. Ever.

**~oOo~**

A few hours later, we arrived at my parents' house. Avidya had let her hair air dry, and the ends were slightly curled. She wore a light pink crocheted sweater over the top of her thin strapped dark blue tank top. The sweater would do nothing to ward off any chill, but only showing off her skin.

I threw on a pair of jeans and a blue shirt, not caring what I wore, as long as it was clean.

"We'll have to try to do this monthly," I mused as I helped her out of the car.

"I'm sure everyone would be up for that," she agreed, laying her head on my arm as we walked up the stone steps.

Like I expected, the front door was opened before we even made it there.

"You are both here sooner than I expected," my

father stated, looking over the both of us.

"Sorry," I shrugged. "We miss our son."

"Good luck getting him away from Toby," Dad spoke, letting us in. "He's not too happy with Melio currently."

"What did he do this time?" Avidya asked, trying, and failing, to hide her amusement.

"Not entirely sure this time," Dad laughed. "I'm staying out of this one."

"Melio, would you knock it off!" Violet said, her voice slightly elevated. As we rounded the corner, I saw what my father was talking about.

My brother, for whatever reason, was trying to use my son as his own personal table as he laid on the floor. There was a small plate now in Toby's hands that had just been on my son's tummy.

"He's perfect size, though," Melio said, trying to take the plate to put it back right where it was.

"Josh is not a table," Toby spoke. Although his voice was quiet, it was filled with disbelief that the grown man could think the way he was.

"He doesn't care. Look at him. He just wants to lay there and do nothing," Melio stated.

"He's a baby," Toby said, looking down at my son.

"He doesn't know what he wants."

"And do you know?" Melio said jokingly. A second later, his smile faded as he realized what he had said. He was worried that Toby would be upset at the words.

I was expecting Toby to clam up, or run away, as he was known to do more times than any of us could count. Violet was ready to jump in at any given moment, but the boy surprised us all. I don't think he knew he had an audience.

"If I was him, I wouldn't want to be used as some piece of furniture," Toby spoke, his voice calm despite his look of hate towards the man he was arguing with. "He's a person. And even though he can't talk, he has the same wants as you. Same as me."

"What are your wants?" Melio asked.

"I want to be happy," Toby said, ducking his head down. "I want a family."

"Oh, Tobs," Melio said, lightly placing his hand on the boy's. "You do have a family here."

"No I don't," Toby said, shaking his head.

"Yes. Yes you do. I won't let you go anywhere else, man. Never. You are as much my son as Josh is Zach's."

I watched in awe as Toby let a small smile fall on his lips. "Can I call you dad, then?"

# Chapter 38
## Avidya

I think Toby surprised everyone. I certainly had never expected him to do that, ever.

"If you want to," Melio said easily. "I would like that, but it's totally up to you."

"Okay," Toby said, not sure what to say. He seemed surprised himself.

Just then, Joshua let out a huge cry, alerting everyone that no one was paying attention to him. My son loved attention, demanded it constantly, too.

The spell was broken as Toby was quick to take my son and hold him, mumbling things to the baby.

"Well that was a good turn out," Violet said on a breath of air. "I expected a huge outburst."

"I think everyone was," I said. "Glad he's doing so much better."

"Thanks to you," Violet said my way. "Whatever you said to him the other day worked wonders."

"I didn't say anything that wasn't true," I shrugged. "He's a good kid. And you and Melio have done wonderful with him."

"We try," Violet said. "He's called me *Mom* a few

times, mostly by accident."

"I don't think it was a mistake. He may have been testing it out to see how you react. You don't jump to conclusions, Vi. Toby knows that and you were a safe person to try it on. I wouldn't have worked for that," I said.

"You're right," she said. "I also think counseling has helped."

"It usually does. It's all about trial and error," I mused.

"When did you grow up?" Violet laughed.

"It's common sense," I blushed.

"Come help me with lunch," Julia called our way.

I gave Zach a shrug, knowing that this was a simple command that she wanted to talk.

Once Violet and I entered the kitchen, Julia didn't waste time is wrapping her arms around us both.

"I can't believe I'm a grandma!" she gushed.

"You've been one since the day we took Toby in," Violet laughed.

"But it's so official!" Julia said, pulling back to wipe at her eyes. "When will you have the documents?"

"We already do. Just have to have a judge sign them and we are all set," Violet stated. Then turning to me, "We've been wanting to adopt Toby, to make him ours once and for all. We just had to wait until he was at the right place to tell him. We love him as though we've always had him."

"That's amazing," I smiled. "You two are great parents."

"Will you take in other kids?" Julia asked.

"Not for another year or more. Toby needs our attention the most right now. Later on down the road, we probably will," Violet answered.

"Will you have any more kids?" Julia asked me. "Zach seems to be great with Josh."

"Not for a while," I answered. "I think one right now is plenty. If it does happen later on, years later, then yes. But right now, we are happy."

"He didn't give you too much of a hard time, did he?" Julia asked.

"Oh, he always does," I smiled. "But nothing I can't handle."

"M…Vi?" Toby asked, entering the kitchen.

"What's up, Toby?" Violet asked, turning around to face Toby.

"Vidie!" he said, spotting me. "I didn't know you were here!"

"Hey, Toby," I said.

A moment later, his arms wrapped around me. I returned his hug.

"You're gonna be my aunt," he said, looking up at me.

"I thought I already was," I winked at him, causing him to roll his eyes at me.

"How do you figure that?" Julia asked.

"Well, she's my aunt," Toby said, fumbling over his words.

"Because you live with Violet and Melio?" I asked.

He nodded his answer.

Even though I knew Violet and Julia most likely could hear me, I whispered to him, "It's okay to call them your parents, you know. They would love it if you did, and they'd never make you call them something they don't want to be called."

He nodded once more against my chest before making his way back out of the room.

"Maybe you should have adopted him instead," Violet laughed.

"I would have if I'd had met Zachariah a year or two before I had. But he's made amazing progress with the two of you," I said. "He'll be a wonderful young man when he grows up."

"That he certainly will be," Julia agreed. "So, switching topics, how about a girls' day out soon. Us three and Kenna?"

"Sure," I agreed. "What about the boys?"

"Josh can stay with Toby and Zach for the day. I think it'd be good for them all," Julia said. "It's amazing that the boy who once feared men adores them, as long as Josh is in the room at least."

"Oh man, Melio keeps goading Toby into arguments constantly!" Violet laughed.

"I do no such thing!" Melio said, entering the kitchen. "Your boy is hungry."

"And let me guess, so are you?" I asked, lifting an eyebrow at my brother in law.

"When isn't he?" Julia laughed.

"Hey!" Melio said, not upset about the statement.

I just shook my head.

Everything really was turning out better than I ever expected it to.

## Chapter 39

### Zachariah

One weekend, a couple of weeks later, I had to leave my son and wife home alone to come in to check on the club.

*Life & Love* was inspired by the women in Travis' and my life. It fit pretty well, now that things were looking up.

Pulling up to the back of the building, which just so happened to be half a mile from the Las Vegas strip, I had to do a double take.

How the heck did Lynn find this place? She wouldn't ever be seen in a place like this, as far as I knew.

After shutting the car off, stepping out, and closing the door, I looked her up and down.

She seemed a little too well put together, considering she was living with less money than she had been a year ago. True, it had been a full year now that she had any contact with anyone in my family. A lot can change in that amount of time.

I knew how true that was.

"What are you doing here, Lynn?" I asked when I

was a few feet from her.

"I'm actually here to talk to you," she said, holding her shoulders back, head held high.

"Go ahead," I waved. There was no way I was going to let her into my building. She was not a member or staff, therefore, not allowed in. My wife would and family would be the only exceptions.

"Can we go inside?" she asked, looking around.

"No one is out here," I hinted. "Here is perfectly fine."

"Fine," she sighed. "How is my daughter?"

"That's not why you are here," I said through clenched teeth. She very well knew that, too. "Either state why you are here, or leave. I will call my security if I have to."

"Who? Travis?" she laughed. "He won't do anything to me."

"Do not test me, Lynn," I seethed, my impatience shining through.

"Fine," she bit out. "I need a place to stay. The guy I was staying with wants money, and I don't have any."

"Then get a job," I huffed. "I'm not bailing you out. Go to a homeless shelter. From the looks of things, he was taking good care of you."

"He…" she began before spotting the man she was staying with as he rounded the corner.

"Gotcha," I laughed, looking between the Dom and this woman.

"There you are, Katty," Master Bruce spoke. "I thought we were meeting at your place to discuss this."

"I thought here would be better," Lynn shrugged, putting on a false smile.

"You want into my club," I guessed. That made sense. She was probably hoping to be taken in by someone that could possibly have a sway in my choices.

"She does," Bruce spoke up. "I'll pay, of course."

"I think we need to talk, first," I stated.

"Oh? About what? I didn't break any rules?" Bruce asked, horrified. I could see that he actually liked this woman for once.

"No, you haven't. I can understand not wanting to use real names inside my place, but if you two met somewhere else you should know. She's not who she says she is," I said, knowing that Lynn would insist to be there as I told this man the truth.

"Katty?" Bruce asked, confused.

"She's the woman who raised my wife. I'll let you two talk. She is never allowed into this club. Personal reasons," I shrugged before unlocking and entering into my building. I left the two grown up people outside, knowing that they would be able to handle it on their own.

"That was interesting," Travis said, popping out of the control room.

That was one thing I didn't skimp out on. I had the most top notch security here. Cameras were in every room, except for the bathrooms and personal rooms. Those, I had speakers in case something happened and I needed to find out for sure the truth of what went on. Cameras were posted on all four corners of my building, too.

"That it was," I said, shaking my head. "She will never learn."

"I think she'll learn now," Travis barked out a laugh. "Maybe she needs a *daddy* to take care of her."

"I never understand how woman like that, but whatever floats their boat," I said as I headed to my office.

"You let them in," Travis yelled after me.

"Doesn't mean I like it," I hollered back.

Life was never boring, that was for sure

Every time I came here, I loved the place more and more. It had a much better layout than the last place I had. It just seemed to be more open, and definitely less cramped when we had parties.

Comparing the two places, this one was twice as big. Had more tables and equipment than I ever thought I would use at first.

I still refused to play here, and likely would never even consider doing so. Then again, maybe one day, I'd bring Avidya here, when she was ready.

One day. One day I'll give her the world if she'll let me.

**Chapter 40**

**Avidya**

**A few years later**

Looking around the house, I couldn't help but be happy with how life turned out to be. It has been six years since I fell in love with Zachariah. Six years of trial and error, but ones I would never want to change.

The house was filled with people, kids, and cowboy decorations as my son had the best fifth birthday he could possibly have. I had to stop his father from renting farm animals and RVs.

Joshua was one determined boy, just like his father. With only being five years old, I could see Zachariah in him more each day. He was his spitting image, except his eye color. He was a handful, too. Thank goodness for family to help keep him busy on the days he needed out of the house. It wasn't that he was a trouble maker, he just got bored so quickly with his toys. He wasn't a fan of TV, mostly because I wouldn't let him sit in front of it for more than a couple of hours a day.

He was the second love of my life, and everyone knew that. It also didn't change the fact that everyone spoiled him rotten every chance they got. I have no idea how he could even want more toys with the room full he had acquired through the years.

"How's my girl doing?" Zachariah asked as he wrapped his arms around me from behind and placed his chin atop my head.

"I'm tired of people," I grumbled, even though the party just started. Josh invited his entire kindergarten class.

"Now, how about my other girl?" he asked, laying a hand across my rounded stomach.

"She wants that strawberry cake your mother brought," I said, turning my head slightly.

"She certainly has a sweet tooth," Zach laughed.

I was seven months pregnant. With a little baby girl. Zach was determined to have one more kid, because he didn't think it was fair to only have one child. I didn't mind, although I was surprised he turned into such a kid magnet.

Now that my husband was a father, or maybe it was just because of Toby, he was trying to be more child friendly. He certainly was not as grumpy as he had once been.

When it came to Toby, though, he was still a little out of his element. Toby was now in in high school, and doing extremely well for how his life had been. He swore off dating anyone, although I secretly thought he had his eyes set on Kenna's niece that had moved in last year with her and Travis.

He had many years of counseling after I returned, because he feared what any man he didn't know would do to him. For his elementary and middle school years, he was home schooled because of his fear. It was understandable, and I couldn't give my sister-in-law enough credit.

Violet and Melio ended up opening their home to a couple more troubled kids, who they loved as their own. None of them were as close as Toby and I were, but I think that had to do with their ages. They were already in their teenage years and wanted nothing to do with anyone.

Kenna and Travis were not trying for any children, instead giving to the community when they could in any way that they could. They got married three years ago, giving each other everything they ever needed.

It really was a happily ever after for everyone. I never thought I'd be this happy. Ever.

Zachariah still ran many businesses and his club while I helped run a daycare not all that far away. I only worked part time while being pregnant, per Zachariah's requests. Joshua thought it was awesome that he got to see some of his friends so much. Toby even helped once in a while.

Toby was going to college to be a child psychologist, and I couldn't be any prouder of him. It was the perfect thing to do. He wanted to help children that were going through what he had.

Toby didn't talk much of his past, preferring to live day to day instead. Surprisingly, he had come along so far after everything.

"How do you think she'll get along in this family?" he asked me as he watched the kids run around the yard.

"She'll be just as spoiled as our son," I laughed, feeling her kick against his hand. "She agrees."

He laughed, too, knowing how right I was.

I knew Zachariah was thrilled that he got to be here every step of the way for this pregnancy, and so was I. It made it all so much more enjoyable this time around.

"Oh my god! Avidya!" Krissy's voice reached me before I saw her. Red hair quickly engulfed me as she pulled me into a bone crushing hug. "I leave for a few months to sell my house, and come back to this?"

"Hi," I breathed out as she released me. But a moment later, Catrina had her arms wrapped around me.

"Another baby? Amazing!" she gushed.

Catrina also had grown up way too fast for my liking. She was now eleven, and turning into an amazing woman.

Krissy and Catrina were moving here to Las Vegas to help run the daycare center. It was Krissy's idea to move because she had nothing tying her back home. Her parents had passed away just two years ago, and nothing was holding her back.

"Kitty!" Josh shouted as he spotted Catrina. He had taken to calling her Kitty because he couldn't say her name when he first started to talk. She didn't care one bit. I thought it was adorable.

"Hey Joshy," she smiled, letting his little arms pull her into a hug.

"She couldn't wait to see him again," Krissy laughed. "So, why did you blow up when I was gone?"

"I didn't," I laughed. "I'm still tiny. You are the one that got bad eyes while gone."

"Oh, shush you," Krissy laughed.

Things never changed between anyone. Not between my friends, and not between my family.

I had once thought that all of this would be so far out of reach, I'd live a crappy life with some nameless man that I would be forced to live with. I never thought I'd have family and friends, and everything else I had I ever wanted right at my fingertips.

I was so happy here; more than I ever thought would be able to.

It was all so much more than I could have asked for.

## Chapter 41

### Toby

I never knew what life could be like. I had never known that there was a family filled with love and peace. I never knew that a family wasn't supposed to turn its back on a child just because of drugs and booze.

I was five years old when I figured out that parents shouldn't be passed out day and night on the couch, leaving a child without food for days.

At the tender of five, social services were called because I was outside filthy from head to toe. Little good that did for me.

My parents, crappy parents at that, put on a great little show to prove that they cared for me. They cleaned the house and made it look 'normal.' How could a house filled with drugs ever look *normal*?

When I was six years old, I gave up any hope. I gave up on the hope that God would come and save me.

My father, when he was home, would hit me, yell at me, and use me in ways that no little boy should ever be used.

Who would I have told? No one would believe a little boy who just wanted attention. I learned that the first and only time I ever said anything.

For years, I suffered abuse at the hands of monsters. It was all I knew.

I wasn't surprised when my father got tired of me. He killed my mother, who had for one single second, tried to get him to leave me alone. That was one single moment that she actually tried to get out, get me out, alive.

I watched through my nine-year-old eyes as my mother bled to death right there in front of me. I watched as her eyes dulled. I watched as she took her last breath as my father kicked her over and over.

I was nine years old, and I never should have had to see that. No child ever should.

I gave up crying. I gave up hope. I gave up trying to live.

What had been the point?

Everyone saw right through me. They didn't even see the real me. No one saw how much pain, inside and out, I held on to.

No ten-year-old should ever think about suicide.

But I wasn't a normal child. I thought about it. And I wanted to end my life just to make the pain stop.

I had no care about what it would do to me. Who cared if I got sent to Hell because I took my life? It had to be better than the Hell I was already living him. Anything had to be better. It had to be.

My father gave me to a man, who in turn gave me to another man. I had no idea where I was, or even why for the most part.

I didn't ask, either. Why? I knew I wouldn't get an answer.

No one wanted me.

I was so sure that when I came into the hands of yet another man with a hard set jaw and face, I would finally find my peace in death. I was sure that he would kill me.

I had been used already in so many ways, I didn't know what was right and wrong anymore.

The only thing I wanted then, was death. Peaceful death.

And I was going to find a way to get just that.

What I hadn't counted on, never even thought about, was coming across a family that actually did care for me.

My hope was entirely gone, crushed into dust and blown away by the strong wind.

But this family, this really odd family, took me in.

They saved me. They gave me a reason to live and keep on trying to breathe day in and day out.

I didn't like men. I couldn't stand to be in the same room as any of them.

Between Avidya and Violet, so much different than any of the men, I never knew what I was missing out on all the years I wanted to die. They showed me a side of life that I never would have known about.

It was because of these two women that I learned that I could have things. I could ask for what I wanted, and speak freely.

I never had to fear being hurt because of something I did. They cared for me like family.

I was part of their family, even if it took me a year to figure that out.

That day, the day I turned twelve, would forever be my favorite day ever. Besides it being my birthday, it was the day I officially became the son of Violet and Melio Melendez. I was their son in just about every way possible.

Now, twenty years old, one would never be able to tell what kind of hell I had gone through in my life. I never expected to live this long. I never would have thought I'd have a family of my own.

Heck, I never thought I would even be doing

something I wanted to do.

After years of trying to figure out how to see the world other than black and white, I finally found myself. So many people helped me along the way, of course. But I would miss and mourn the childhood that I never got to have.

And I was okay with that. I still had a life to live and other lives to change.

When I first started school, I was so far behind. I could just barely read a few things here and there that I had taught myself. I had to read a little bit just so I could try to not be hit and taken advantage of so much.

Little good that did anyhow.

So when Violet sat me down to see where I was with school, I expected her to hate how far behind I was. I expected her to scream, and maybe even kick me out.

None of that happened.

Instead, she bought everything she possibly could and taught me herself. She showed me how much fun learning really was, and not to fear what I had no control over.

Because of the care and time my new adopted mother took, I went far and wide with learning. I was like a sponge after knowing I could learn all sorts of information.

I had a great memory, which helped. I don't make a huge deal out of it, because it's just who I am.

Once I turned sixteen, I was determined to try high school. I was so nervous. I was scared no one would be my friend. Or worse, I worried that my past would become my present.

I made a number of great friends who didn't care about my past. The teachers did everything they could to make me feel comfortable and safe. It took a few weeks before all that happened, but it did.

Since everyone was so helpful, so encouraging, I was able to test out of high school a year yearly.

It's not often I can surprise myself, but I did it!

I have no idea what life will have in store for me next, but I'm ready for whatever it may be. Maybe someday I'll find the love of my life. Maybe I'll become a foster parent, just like my own parents.

As long as I can help just one person.

I'm going to college to become a therapist. One of which that will stand up for abused children. I don't care if I have to stand in front of a hundred people to prove that a child had been abused. I would do anything to make sure that children knew there is a way out besides death. I will show them that the world is filled with both good people.

I know I have my work cut out for me, but after everything I've been through, I can do this.

I can take on the entire world and live.

I am Toby Melendez, and I will make a difference.

One person at a time.

66032195R00182

Made in the USA
Lexington, KY
01 August 2017